# AUTUMN'S GRACE

"This book is the healing that Mother Earth and our beautiful country need right now. As Frances embarks on her healing journey through self-reflection, connecting to the land, and cultural teachings, she outlines a path our country can take to heal from the intergenerational trauma of Native people throughout our history. This path includes remembering herself as Blue Jaguar, letting go of anger, and forgiving those who have caused the anger. It prioritizes remembering our heart. Frances recognizes the sacredness of the earth and prescribes, 'The many are one for what lies before us.' She urges us to find what unites us. Everyone needs to hear this message of healing going forward."

- Bobbi Rahder, retired museum director of Stewart Indian School Museum & Cultural Center

"*Autumn's Grace* is an epic story full of heart, vulnerability, and courage—with a side of chingona. Lorraine Martinez-Cook writes with poetic lyricism, weaving herself into every page. Like Spider Woman in the book's opening creation story, she spins a world of healing, memory, and transformation. Frances, her protagonist, mirrors Lorraine's own journey through loss, joy, and a profound reckoning with the self— told through the voice of an elder Wisdom Keeper. This novel carries the same grit, grace, and humor that its author embodies. Lorraine is a powerful storyteller and medicine woman whose 'good heart and untamable soul' illuminate the narrative. A must-read for anyone seeking authentic stories that are courageous, rooted, and spiritually alive."

- Deborah Najman, M.A. Depth Psychology, specializing in community, liberation, indigenous, and eco psychologies, Ph.D. candidate

"*Autumn's Grace* is a woman's journey fueled by the wind with love, insight, truth, softness, fierceness, and surprises. This is a must-read if you are a woman who wants to go deeper into who and what you are, as defined by you. Open your heart and spirit to being inspired and empowered from the inside out."

- Dr. Anita Sanchez, Nahua Aztec and Toltec, podcast host and author of *The Four Sacred Gifts*

"Women who are grappling with owning their own wisdom and power will value the story and rich lessons of *Autumn's Grace*."

- Leslie A. Pritchett, leader in collaborative art programming

"In *Autumn's Grace*, we experience a window into the soul of a warrior woman living in these times, grounded in wisdom of countless generations. Her path lets us see the world through honest, soulful reflection and the growth we each may attain through looking inward toward spirit. Fierce and loving, she shares her delicious spirit with equal measures of joy and sorrow."

- Christopher Tennis, Ph.D., organizational development consultant for Sanchez, Tennis & Associates, LLC

"*Autumn's Grace* takes you on a beautiful journey. Weaving Indigenous and Chicana experiences, giving the reader a glimpse of cultures not everyone gets to experience. The realism and magic are felt through the pages. I highly recommend it, as it is a great read and reminder for women to stand in their truth."

- Cynthia M. Ruiz, Cherokee Latina, author and professor

"Lorraine Martinez-Cook opens a window into a world older than the USA and a culture dismissed by many in the mainstream of Americana. Step into the shoes of Frances as she navigates through the challenges of two cultures: one that views people as stewards of the Earth and its bounty, the other that sees the natural world as something to be exploited for profit. In a land where freedom of independent action is often prioritized over the collective good, she observes that everything is connected, so there is no escape from 'the ripples your actions created,' and she does not spare those who fail to see this reality. Through this book, we can learn these same lessons and more when we join her in this spiritual journey."

- Thomas K. Pendergast, media journalist

"In *Autumn's Grace*, this first-time author gifts us with a story not often told ... the story of a woman in the 'autumn' of her life. A woman who, through the embrace of her indigenous culture(s) realizes that her life experience has helped her to see herself more clearly as she is able to shed her anger and accept what is. It shows her what to keep and what to shed as no longer useful. Her true authentic self has emerged like a phoenix, and that is a triumph! Bravo!"

- Paulette Fiorina, activist and advocate for foster children

"One takeaway is that it's never too late to learn and grow. Frances is a complex character trying to find truth and meaning in a world that sometimes seems to be exploding and sometimes is closing in on her. At age 75, the protagonist of this intricately woven tale of self-discovery finally is able to embrace her indigenous heritage and her spirituality without fear or regret. Lorraine Martinez-Cook has done a nice job of blending all the diverse elements together to chart Frances's various epiphanies as she works her way toward making peace with herself and her place in the larger scheme of things.

- Ronald Hurlburt, retired literary professor

"*Autumn's Grace* invites the reader to join her on a journey of healing and discovery. Frances shares her life without apology and with an unbiased truth. She shares her story as a true chingona. I so enjoyed the journey."

- Jennie Estrada, medicine woman, Latina, author and chingona

"*Autumn's Grace* is a journey unfolding in the life of a modern day medicine woman giving the reader insight into the struggles and victories of a healer."

- Shelly Hill, student accessibility services and testing coordinator, Embry-Riddle Aeronautical University

# AUTUMN'S GRACE

*a novel*

## LORRAINE MARTINEZ-COOK

Copyright © 2025 by Lorraine Martinez-Cook

All rights reserved.

Edited by: Elizabeth Gudrais
Cover and interior design by: Andrea Gibb
Author photo by: Steve Lucero Photography

To contact the author or for permission requests, please email: lo55rraine@gmail.com.

ISBN 978-1-957408-21-7 (paperback)
ISBN 978-1-957408-22-4 (ebook)

Library of Congress Control Number: 2025908825

Published by Awaken Village Press,
Sioux Falls, South Dakota, U.S.A.
www.awakenvillagepress.com

*All those loved ones who have gone before me, you are forever in my heart.*

| | |
|---|---|
| *"A qué?"* | "A what?" (Spanglish expression) |
| *barrio* | Neighborhood |
| *channunpa* | Lakota name for the sacred ceremonial pipe used in their ceremonies |
| *chingona* | Strong, independent, badass, awesome, damn cool woman |
| *chola* | Mexican-American gangsta girl |
| *comadre* | Your children's godmother or a close friend with a lifelong bond |
| *con mucho respeto* | With much respect |
| *cuidate* | Take care of yourself |
| *curandera* | Indigenous healer |
| *ese* | Dude, man |
| *gente* | People |
| *heyoka* | A sacred clown or jester, often acting as a spiritual teacher and trickster |
| *Inipi* | Sweat lodge ceremony |
| *kinnek-kinnek* | A traditional Native American and First Nations herbal smoking mixture |
| *loca* | Crazy woman |
| *maestra* | Woman teacher |

| | |
|---|---|
| *manzanita* | Evergreen shrub native to western North America *(Arctostaphylos)* |
| *nada* | Nothing |
| *OG* | Original gangster (often used to describe someone who is considered a pioneer, expert, or authentic in a particular field) |
| *órale* | Common term in Mexican-American culture used as a greeting or to express agreement |
| *pachucas* | A Mexican-American youth subculture during a time of increased racism and the fight for rights and equality within American society (during the 1930s zoot suit era) |
| *pendejo/a* | Moron (with different forms for a man or a woman) |
| *pinche* | Fuckin' worthless, cheap |
| *puto* | A vulgar insult toward a man |
| *quinceañera* | A traditional Mexican celebration marking a girl's fifteenth birthday and her transition from childhood to womanhood |
| *tía* | Aunt |
| *tierra* | Land |
| *Turtle Island* | A name used by some Indigenous peoples to refer to North America, particularly the continent's landmass |
| *yaguara azul* | Blue jaguar |
| *vamos* | Let's go |

It was the time of purple. Spider Woman closed her eyes and began to hum her incantations. Tones weaved themselves around her and comforted her in her nothingness. It was pure and undiluted joy. Spider Woman inhaled and paused, then exhaled and paused. In the pauses she could hear the drumbeat of her heart, quiet and rhythmic. She let her vivid insight flow for a while before she opened her eyes.

All Spider Woman saw was the unknown before her. So she decided to reach into her navel and pull out a bright star so she could see what she was about to create. She decided to call this bright, glowing star the Sun. Now everything before her was bright and lit up. The first thing she saw were her hands and how beautiful they were. She flexed her delicate fingers and rubbed her thumbs across them. She clapped her hands together and began laughing. She was excited to begin a new project for herself. This one felt special. This one felt colorful. This one could be felt deep in her belly where a woman creates from.

With the Sun's powerful rays assisting her, Spider Woman began her work. She could see every detail. She reached into her medicine handbag that carried all the possibilities. As she felt around, her fingers settled on a round object, and she pulled it out. A circle of energy rested on the palms of her hands. Her passion created the color red, and the orb began to absorb this. Her passion grew so strong it created heat too hot to handle, and she let go of the sphere.

Spider Woman tried again as she reached for another orb. This time, she imagined something much cooler, and a hint of blue encircled the orb. As she watched it with an austere demeanor, ice volcanoes began to form on its surface. Although they were pretty to look at, she felt her palms begin to freeze—so she tossed the orb into the vat of space and time.

What she desired in her two hearts—the heart in her chest and the heart in her belly—was a place of abundance. A place that breathed like her. A place that sang like her. A place that danced like her. A place that stretched like her. A place that traveled like her. A place that grew like her. A place that cared like her. A place that loved like her. A place that honored itself. Was that too much to ask?

Spider Woman continued for some time to create all colors of spheres—each one an experiment—by adding different ingredients from her handbag. One formed beautiful rings around itself. She watched it and poked it a little bit. Some formed little spheres that danced around the larger sphere. All were beautiful; however, being the woman she was and being determined to get it just right, she continued to work on her project.

Each sphere was a lesson, and she listened to her intuition as she created the tones of turquoise she was seeking. Not too hot; not too cold. Not too dark; not too light. Not too hard; not too soft. Not too brittle; not too pliable. Just right.

She recognized that the elements she was using to shape and form her art piece would need the right balance. A palmful of water. Clay and minerals to give it some body. A pinch of fire to give it life. Spider Woman tried this approach and watched it morph. It seemed like something was missing.

Spider Woman instinctively smiled and began to gently offer her sacred breath to this sphere. As it began to spin, it developed the verdant zones of life she knew could be possible. The sphere began to vibrate in tones of resplendent turquoise and violet. All the colors of the spectrum danced around this orb. She saw the hints of its potentiality sparkle before her. This was the sphere she felt most alive with.

From this revelation, she began to offer her breath to all the other spheres floating around. Spider Woman realized her sacred breath would be what was needed for all the spheres to grow in their own sovereignty. Quietly, the spheres began to circle the great star, the Sun.

Spider Woman watched with her hands held together and wondered at this beauty before her. She took it in and reflected a deep knowledge from her own experiences that everything is ephemera, everything is in flux, everything is in motion—that all she could do for her creation of this solar system was to let it grow and let it go. So she offered it to the forces of nature. Spider Woman gathered her strength, knowing the seeds she planted here were from her formidable heart and soul. A good heart. An untamable soul.

As she watched the spheres circle the Sun, Spider Woman was

happy, and she began to hum her soul music. She reached into her handbag for her rattle and added words to her music. The spheres began to dance around the Sun in harmony with each other. This was more than she had hoped for.

And life as we know it began . . .

# TONANTZIN'S BLESSINGS

Frances found herself in an unfamiliar place—completely new territory, no map, no instructions, no guidance—yet, it felt so good to be here. It was 2021, and Frances was feeling every year since her birth seventy-five years earlier, and it felt fresh. Feeling clear and concise had become her new compass. It felt illuminated and colorful; it was a good direction for her.

Everything may have looked the same as before Frances's transition, but all things tangible had a certain elevated vibrancy. She even felt thirty pounds lighter without losing a pound … or perhaps she had? It didn't matter. Her skin and hair felt softer than before. She noticed that she'd begin cracking up at the silliest little things. Flashes of her childlike sense of wonder popped up, and she felt free to pursue her curiosities.

She listened more than she had before, heard the breezes slide by her body and in the distance. She sat with birds in her backyard and opened her ears to their language of song. She wondered whether roots made sounds, so she laid her ear down on the ground and listened to the underground sound of the Earth. It was delightful, like listening to the inside of a seashell and hearing the echoes of the ocean.

Her practical self had been diminished when she'd begun to surrender to exhaustion after all those years of carrying the heavy suitcase of her hidden anger. In her recovery, she rested more deeply and gave herself more time to do so. Her dreams became wonder landscapes—surrealism at its best. She woke up without frustration, without wondering or analyzing hidden messages. The new dreams spoke very clearly of resolutions and potential for her days ahead. They were fresh and crisp, like a delicious salad nurturing her psyche.

Frances began to recognize that her spiritual self had been kicked up a notch by the sensitivities of her intuitive self instead of the external world she had been so focused on. Her reluctance to embrace her spiritual name, given to her in a naming ceremony prior to the pandemic, was diminishing. She had been struggling to feel worthy of such a beautiful name because of the responsibility it implied. It would mean she would have to put the spiritual shoes on and walk the talk.

Even her way of eating had changed. No longer was she obsessed with strict rules of eating healthy and avoiding her old-time comfort and favorite foods. It didn't matter any longer if they were considered nutritional taboos. Savoring and tasting every note of flavor with small, delicate bites made her feel free to enjoy. She had always had an affinity for sweets, but now her selection became refined. If it was too sugary, she just spit it out. One bite of a delicacy was all she needed to feel that glow within. Eating was no longer a pathway to her aging health but, rather, a sensuous relationship with food of all types. She scoffed at the large portions served at restaurants, knowing she would have plenty of leftovers for the week ahead.

The weight of fearlessness replaced the doubts she had carried around. The ominous messages of news headlines no longer triggered her. Divisive politics of her nation no longer concerned her. Her radical views toward mean people became softened with compassion for those who suffered deep wounds of their own.

It became apparent to her that her superhuman power of seeing lies float around people had sprouted another level of growth. This power was something she had carried her entire life, and it had served her as a warning sign, but now she saw the luggage others carried as well—the luggage of their wounds. It didn't make her sad, just aware. She learned to witness rather than engage. She knew that she could not save the entire fucking planet. She could only be an example of her own values. The ones with an atomic thread of compassion seemed to be working for her now.

All that she had gone through in the past several months had an effect on her. Frances had chosen to isolate herself during the pandemic of Covid. She'd dismissed her own safety concerns and taken chances that she wasn't totally comfortable with.

It was in the chaos of these intense adventures that she'd met incredible new allies—allies who had witnessed her heartbreak and encouraged her to get up and notice the integrity of people all around her. She had been given a gift of grace that she'd absorbed all the way to her bones.

There was one particular gentleman who had emerged as a solid human being: a rancher who went by the name of Theodore. He had found her stranded with a flat tire on a gravel road out on the south end of Pine Ridge when she'd driven into town with her friend's granddaughter to pick up some ice. He had pulled over to help her, and during her adventure there in South Dakota, they'd developed a good friendship. He had texted her a few times to make sure she was safe as she'd headed home to Nevada after leaving Pine Ridge. She had forgotten her prayer shawl at the ceremony she'd attended, and he had retrieved it for her. In their correspondence, she had told him to hold on to it and that she would get it the following year; she planned on returning to pray in this special way of her native ancestors. She didn't want her shawl mailed to her because it imbued the beauty of her prayers; she trusted him to take good care of it.

It was late summer now, and she missed her family. She decided one more road trip was necessary for her well-being, and her other home—the home of her family—was calling her back. She would drive south from northern Nevada along the eastern Sierras to her City of Angels, with no agenda but to be safe in the waning days of Covid's grip on society. She planned to wear her mask and provide her vaccination card for entry into public places in case her presence was questioned. A few days before heading south to Los Angeles, Frances was backing out of her garage when a text came in. It was from Theodore, her rancher friend.

Theodore: Hi, what's up?

Frances: Hey, it's you! Heading south in a couple of days.

Theodore: Where to?

Frances: My ol' stomping grounds.

Theodore: Occasion?

Frances: None, just miss my family, some homemade Mexican food and my favorite beach.

Theodore: Never been to the ocean

Frances: Whaaaat? Oh you need to see it, feel it, smell it, taste it, hear it!

Theodore: Is that an invitation?

Frances: If you want it to be. It's a long drive from S. Dakota

Theodore: Perhaps

Frances: How are you?

Theodore: Staying busy

Frances: Ranch work?

Theodore: Always something to work on

Frances: Good to hear from you

Theodore: Yeah, thinking about you. Have a safe trip. No more flat tires!

Frances: Ha! Sure

The highway to her family connected her to that place of her past. She had driven this road for years. On this day of her current road trip, however, she noticed a lack of other vehicles on the road. Maybe the threat of Covid was still on people's minds, or maybe it was the outrageous gas prices that affected the West Coast more than other parts of the country. As the clouds paraded north in a slow procession, scraping the peaks of the Sierras, she felt the headwinds against her truck—a challenging resistance. She was tempted to make her foot heavier on the accelerator, yet her usual habit of driving exactly at the speed limit seemed to stretch out before her and expand her drive. There were forests to cross, lakes to absorb, raptors to soar with. In her resistance to go faster, it took her all day and early evening to cross over the line into L.A. County.

The tangle of freeways, each with its own destination—a big asphalt knot that presented itself as gates to the metropolis—could confuse anyone, with or without a GPS. After the long slow-motion drive, Frances adjusted her mindset, automatically reverting to the driving tactics of her youth and slicing right through the traffic as she made her way toward her destination. Traffic pulsed, weaved, and flowed without triggering her this time.

Arriving at her *tía*'s house, she surrendered to being gathered in a circle of hugs as her relatives had always done. This time, she allowed herself to absorb it completely, as the walls around her were gone. They had missed her too, and it touched her formidable heart. The homemade foods on the dining room table rekindled her sweet youth with familiar flavors. She found herself laughing and having no expectations of anyone around her. These new shoes she walked in had freed her of resentment toward her past. She wondered how anything could possibly get better than this as she took notice of the apparent change within.

As Frances's visit continued, this state of contentment amplified. Her state of happiness was mirrored by everyone around her. Everything felt spontaneous as the city itself reached out to her. She passed by parks that held good memories of birthdays and picnics shared. The strip malls that now covered fields could not erase the grove of trees they'd replaced, where she had once swung from a rope swing like a fearless monkey. The American Legion Hall that had held her reception for her *quinceañera* was a bit rundown but still there. Her heart smiled to remember the crazy times of her youth. She realized as she drove around El Sereno, the neighborhood she'd grown up in, that no matter how challenging her growth process had been nor the environment that had witnessed that growth, it was her very own university of hard knocks and rocks—her temple of knowledge and wisdom—that ultimately supported her integrity. On this visit, she could see the good times that had paled in comparison to the pain of all that she'd lost there. The loss of her parents, of her first love lost in Vietnam, of schoolmates to drugs and gang violence. It was the *barrio*, after all.

Frances had been in contact with Lillian, her best friend from her preschool days, and one morning a text from Lillian popped up.

Lillian: Hi Hon. Wanna dance tonight, downtown, under the stars and full moon? Music Center. I'll pick you up at 5. Let me know.

Frances: Music Center? Is it dressy? And yes I can.

Lillian: No, summer casual. It's an outdoor event facing City Hall. I'm bringing my granddaughter some homemade quiche, champagne. It will be fun. So glad you said yes last minute.

Frances: Can I bring anything? Sounds like a hoot. ♥ What kind of music?

Lillian: Doesn't matter. We dance tonight! Pick up some strawberries! Cookies!

Later that afternoon, as Frances waited out on the front porch for Lillian to arrive, her phone buzzed with an incoming text. It was Theodore from South Dakota.

Theodore: I have a surprise!

Frances: Hey you! What's up?

Theodore: I made it

Seeing Lillian pull up, Frances responded without taking the time to process what Theodore had written.

Frances: Sorry my friend just arrived. We're going downtown L.A. to the Music Center for an outdoor event. I'll text you later?

Theodore: Sure, enjoy.

The street was wide in front of Tía Esther's home, and Lillian parked with plenty of room, leaving the driver's side door wide open as she exited the car. In the moment she made eye contact with Frances, gratitude was transmitted for their history together—so many years and experiences shared, the ebbs and flows of life together. The graduations, the marriages, the celebrations, the funerals, the dinners, the sorrows, and the joys; this particular joy they both felt in the present because several years had passed since they'd last seen each other.

Frances and Lillian had decided when they were children that they would be *comadres*—godmothers, or, in a literal translation of the term, co-mothers, to each other's firstborn children. Although Frances did not have children of her own, she held this role of *comadre* with esteem and high honor and extended it to Lillian's grandchildren as well. Trust was imperative because it involved the most beloved thing in one's life: their child. Through all the trials and tribulations of life, a *comadre* could match the strength of any mountain. Now, Lillian walked around the back of her car to open the door and unbuckle a child in the backseat. As the child came into view, Frances saw a miniature of her *comadre*.

The little girl had just turned five and had long dark hair and a cute smile. As her grandmother helped her out of her seat and onto the pavement, Frances took notice of the little girl's exuberant curiosity toward her. She wore a red summer dress with caramel-colored leather sandals. Frances noticed that the girl was wearing lipstick in a color that matched her own; she felt a sense of familiarity connecting them even though they were strangers.

"Well, I'm so honored to meet you, Valerie!" said Frances as she extended her hand out and curtsied.

The little girl giggled and responded with a curtsy too. "Yes, you are my grandma's friend. We have the same color lipstick! My grandma said I could wear it for a special time."

"I'm so excited to dance with you and Grandmother Moon," Frances offered.

The little girl looked at her own grandmother and questioned with her eyes. Grandmother Moon?

Lillian answered instinctively: "Yes, some people call the moon Grandmother."

Valerie put her finger on her cheek and asked, "Why?"

Lillian looked at Frances and said, "Do you want to answer that?"

Frances replied, "Because the moon is loving and beautiful like grandmas are."

All the girls hugged each other at the same time, and Lillian said, "Okay, *vamos!* Get in the car."

Frances's *comadre* knew exactly where she was going as she made turns on specific back streets in order to reach the heart of the city. The drive there did not include freeways. As they passed by neighborhoods, parks, schools, hospitals, warehouses, and historic districts like Clover, Dogtown, and Chinatown, Frances's memories went whizzing by. So much had changed in sixty or more years, yet the foundation of her existence remained intact. Her eyes lingered for a moment as they passed Olvera Street with its restaurants and wooden kiosks beneath colorful pastel flags that draped across the rooftops; the street reminded Frances of her Chicana heritage and pride.

Getting to the underground parking required another level of expertise that only Angelenos could navigate with precision. Every turn Lillian made was deliberate, crossing one-ways to head in a direction toward the entrance. The last thing Frances saw before they took a dip beneath the surface was the towering phallic symbol of Los Angeles City Hall.

Parking was available next to the stairs, and Lillian claimed her spot. They gathered at the trunk of the car to retrieve the picnic basket and sweaters. As they climbed up one flight to street level, the sunset's bright hues engulfed them. "This way," said Frances's *comadre*, and they followed.

As Frances's eyes adjusted, next to the staircase, she saw something so familiar that it took her breath away. *Hey, wait a minute*, she thought to herself as she remembered being here in another time. She gravitated toward the walls of glass and spotted the chandeliers—yes, the same ones of her tender years, sparkling as always. She beheld the Dorothy Chandler Pavilion, the very same elegant place where she'd performed with the school orchestra in her elementary school days. Music was her joy, and the city was once again reminding her of the good times of her youth.

"Hey, come on, over here," the li'l one yelled out as Frances lingered.

Frances turned around and caught up with them. In the area in front of the stage, outdoor boutique tables were set out, and her *comadre* claimed the bright red one with four chairs near the sectioned dance floor. Lillian pulled out the checkered tablecloth from the basket and smoothed it out over the table; the wrapped quiche and plates followed. Valerie helped to make it pretty, showing her cultivated upbringing with her knowledge of how to set a table. The last thing to come out was the champagne from the small ice chest.

The little girl sat down on her chair across from Frances; her grandmother poured a glass of apple juice and handed it to her. As the full moon began to light up the eastern horizon behind City Hall, the girls raised their glasses and toasted to the evening. Something about it felt staged, as though their picnic items were props in an opera. As the pastel hues of pink and orange to the west made the blue lights outlining the iconic City Hall appear more vibrant, other skyscrapers began to light up and reveal their own roles in this real-life staged production.

Taking his cue from the sky, the event's emcee began an invocation, starting with a land acknowledgement thanking the Tongva People—the first peoples of the Los Angeles basin—for their generations of stewardship of the land, their sacrifice of resources to a modern world, and their spiritual presence. The unseen ancestors of this place were finally being given respect. As Frances gathered her hands to her heart, the li'l one followed her gesture, and they smiled to one another.

The music began, and all three of them joined the people from all walks of life on the dance floor. Together. Dancing. All keeping their distance, concealing their smiles behind masks, yet revealing rays of joy from the corners of their eyes. The girls danced until the moon took her position above their heads.

Here, at the sacred ground of Frances's seed origin, with the hospital of her birth just across the freeway, she felt that she recognized herself for the first time in years.

Just then, something familiar caught the corner of her eye. She immediately recognized the lavender fringe of her prayer shawl draped over Theodore's forearm. As recognition came over her and her eyes traveled up the arm to his face, she saw him standing there smiling.

She remembered the words from his text—"I made it"—and realized what he had meant. He was here. She looked up—toward the moon, opened, surrendered, vulnerable—and then down to see the spiritual shoes of her given name that she was ready to walk in.

*The unforeseen forces of her spirit animal
initiated its traits onto her:*

A dream of serpents

Cosmic serpents and serpents of the sea

From an aerial they look like rivers

Long and smooth

But I know better

In this dream

A reflection of my destiny

This serpent has appeared to me

For reasons unknown

– Frances Refugio Reyes

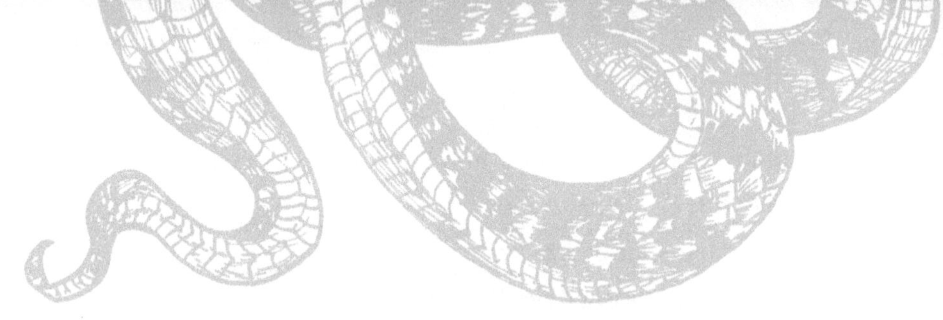

# BECLOUDED EYES

Frances had just gotten back in her truck to drive home when she heard the bells of message notifications ringing on her phone. She felt a flash of annoyance as she glanced down at her phone and saw new messages in real time pop up in the Women's Circle thread. She was having trouble pinpointing the cause of her emotion. Was it anger, ego, or her basic need to defend herself?

It was 2020, the year before she arrived at her state of grace, and Frances was struggling with the uncertainty of a world gripped by the crisis of Covid-19. She tried to navigate with common sense, yet her world felt upside down. Her patience was thin, her fears and frustration real as she watched news reports of increasing numbers of people dying from week to week with no end in sight. Technology seemed to be her only outlet during this time of social isolation, yet learning to use these newfangled tools wasn't always easy for her.

Reading the text thread again, Frances felt heat from her body begin to swallow her. She reminded herself that she had just left a healing session and was coming out with her heart wide open and tender. Participants had shared about their experiences on the beach, their love for life, their exhilaration at witnessing a rainbow. The love this circle professed was not something Frances was feeling at this particular moment.

She had joined the Women's Circle not only in hopes of generating income—it had appealed to her entrepreneurial spirit—but also as a way to connect with the community. In the early days of the pandemic, she had shut down everything she'd worked so hard to build. Frances's small business of spreading wellness by selling the harvest from her garden or facilitating energy work suddenly felt too risky. She was in her seventies now, and she knew she was at risk of being hospitalized if she contracted the virus. Her world became smaller—until the online world presented her with new horizons.

Frances recalled how the Zoom meeting host had said this was the time for all voices to be heard, that everything shared in this circle would be respected. She had written a simple question on the text thread—"Could someone join this circle by Western Union?"—and had received a response that felt like mockery.

She had read somewhere online that these circles were practiced in developing countries for people who did not have access to banks and credit cards—women empowering each other and supporting each other's dreams—so it had seemed like a reasonable question.

Rereading the response, she felt bitch-slapped by rudeness in real time. "It would possibly delay me by weeks."

Where was this coming from? Frances wasn't asking about sending checks or money orders in the mail. She thought to herself, *Wait—I thought this was a safe place to ask questions?*

"I didn't even know what WU was. Had to look it up," the group leader's response continued. A simple "no" would have sufficed.

Frances's internal response had a deep tone of rage: "Really?

You're so technically advanced, bitch?" Beginning to see this circle for something different than she had initially thought, Frances mused, *Ohhh, right—it's a circle of privilege and entitlement! Must be nice to be so young and hip.*

She turned down the radio and asked herself, *What happened? How was I such a fool? What was I thinking?*

Her grand assumption of trust in strangers shrank into shriveled raisins. The *kumbaya* language they had used in the text had sucked her in, and she hadn't even seen it coming. It was because of her need to believe in collaboration and because she wanted this Women's Circle to work. It was that very real place she needed at this moment.

Frances felt her heart begin to pump a bit faster as she stepped on the clutch and shifted the gear into reverse. She wanted to reply right away, but had not yet developed the skill of multitasking, so she drove south on the highway and waited until she approached the next red light to lift up her phone.

Now, there was another comment: "I don't even know how to go about using WU here in Tulum. So if I contribute that way, I'm already lost."

Frances was losing hope that this group could be a place of understanding and open-minded discovery if such a simple conversation was going so badly off the rails. She hadn't been asking about Western Union being required, only about it being a possibility. The light turned green, and she drove on.

When Frances drove, she was focused on the road, on the clutch and the gears she needed to shift. Automatic transmissions made for an insipid experience, detracting from the art of driving with their dashboard computer screens, back-up warning cameras, and all the other automatic driving apparatus installed in them. Frances needed a manual transmission. It felt like being in harmony with the power of an engine, a motor responding to the palm of her hand and the bottom of her foot at the same time. It was a dance she had cultivated over the years. Solid and good, she enjoyed her ride through life.

She didn't even miss having GPS. She would use instinct and her sense of direction to find her way around the streets of cities or, in rural areas, would use landmarks like mountains, valleys, and rivers. It was a game for her to find what she was looking for. So what if she got lost? Fuck it—that was her attitude.

The question about Western Union continued to occupy her thoughts. She supposed it was somewhat of a relic, an earlier form of money exchange. She was asking a generation whose lives were ruled by Venmo, PayPal, and CashApp. They wanted instant dollars with no routing numbers or trips to the bank.

Frances shifted into high gear and kept her speed up for a while, mulling over this situation. The concept of an online community was not that far-fetched for her. Her salt-and-pepper hair did not stop her from experimenting with life. She was always trying new things she knew nothing about. It was like being attracted to pretty little shoes: You had to try them on for fit before you determined whether or not they hurt your feet.

This particular circle of prosperity Frances had decided to join used language involving the elements to give it a hip vibe: earth, wind, fire, water. To Frances, this was a band she had listened to growing up. When the song "September" played at weddings, she would automatically gravitate toward the dance floor and jam with the tunes. Shit, she had been familiar with these terms before anybody on the text thread was born! She knew that for a fact. She could tell by their language and how they'd reacted to her question. She noticed that she was beginning to turn into the one who judges, feeling the switch as she began to downshift approaching the next red light. She tried not to be judgmental toward others, but her anger was unleashed now.

The comments continued to accumulate. "I think it would slow things down considerably if we have to use Western Union," someone else had written. "Curious what others think?"

Frances lost her place on the thread as she glanced ahead at the road. It would take some time for her to get to the next signal; since the highway was dark and unsafe to pull over, she decided to pull into the next gas station for a beverage and top off her tank. The first thing she did after parking was pick up her phone so she could start from the beginning of the thread instead of glimpsing pieces here and there.

"Happy to have you here in this space and to be traveling onwards with all of you!" (Followed by emojis of a rainbow, stars, and a yellow kissing face.)

"Feels like we are really shifting something today. After I said yes to join, I went to the beach for a swim. And there was a whole rainbow and a second one starting. It was pure magic." (Star, hibiscus, heart, exclamation mark.)

"Hey sisters"… "I'm thrilled"… "So many blessings"… "sacred space"…

Frances scrolled some more and came upon a text she had missed the first time. "Apparently, we can go to Cancun to use WU in Mexico, but it's an expensive taxi ride and would take half the day. As a single mom with a business, I would have to schedule that trip out by at least a week or two, arrange babysitting, and so on."

Frances could not believe how this one person in Tulum could not let it go. A simple question had sparked overwhelming resistance over one person's inconvenienced lifestyle. How self-centered this person sounded, trying to get others' validation on the thread.

Frances held off from commenting on the thread just yet, but she couldn't restrain her inner dialogue. *Did that li'l bitch just say it would take her half a day to pick up my money? Perhaps spending time with your kid on a taxi ride to town might be a good experience? Or are they an inconvenience to you too? H'mm this younger generation can kiss my ass.*

She pondered whether to give the thread more time to demonstrate the hypocrisy of the prosperity circle. Her impulse was to shred them a new asshole—a response she was all too comfortable with. She considered using guilt or shame to remind them of the original tenets of the Women's Circle. Trust, community, dignity, empowerment, support, flow—there were too many words for her to use as a hook.

As she continued her long drive home, her thoughts began to drum up her appreciation for the value of her own time, her own value of respect, her own value of integrity. She felt the gap between the generations and wondered about being involved at all.

If only they knew her. That was it—they didn't even know her. They didn't know she worked hard on the land, drove a tractor, and grew flowers and vegetables. They didn't know she enjoyed her relative abundance, that she relished in her friendships and the laughter that followed. That her word meant something deep, that integrity helped her navigate the obstacles of life. She felt comfortable with that vantage point: If only they knew her. If only they had shown a little respect toward an elder.

She wanted to tell these youngsters, in their so-called safe space, that she was a woman who had experienced a long continuum of time, who had lived the extreme ebb and flow of existence. She had witnessed the turbulent times of Vietnam, the assassinations of the Kennedys and Martin Luther King. That Haight-Ashbury was a real experience, not just a video. She was old enough to have seen Jimi Hendrix and Janis Joplin live. The *barrio* that had schooled her was the crucible of her soul. It had taken her years to develop as a woman, a friend, and a healer—and yet she was given no respect at all. She was in her crone phase as a woman and wanted to share her wisdom, but it seemed like she was being discounted because of a simple question some found unreasonable.

It seemed as if the importance of rapid payment was overruling the compassion others were willing to show her on the discussion thread. Frances wondered if this young woman even knew the language of Mexico. Was she one of those expats who distanced themselves from the true people of the land, or were indigenous people perhaps limited to being servants in her household? Was this person one of those who became elitist in their lifestyle of vegetarianism, yoga, healing, love and light? Someone exuding compassion that only extended to her own kind?

After years of practicing energy work, Frances had become familiar with this type of immature woman who offered everyone gifts of love and light, operating with her head in the clouds and a lack of grounding. Frances would just shake her head, knowing the shadow of arrogance was waiting to meet up with them just around the corner. She could warn them, but she couldn't understand it for them.

She wanted to tell the women that she couldn't care less about the speed of their technology, that she found it hilarious to have conversations with young people who felt it was necessary to Google facts mid-sentence. It was obvious to her how insecure they were, how dependent on their technology. Who were they without their smartphones? Who were they, really?

Approaching her driveway, Frances gripped the bottom of her steering wheel and turned her truck onto the gravel road. She parked and turned everything off, wondering: What was her next step?

She lit a cigarette and stared ahead toward the crescent moon descending over the mountain peak and a bright planet nearby. In this quiet moment, her heart spoke, and she heard that her desire to trust strangers in her new adventure overrode the sting involved. She reflected on her anger and wondered if she was becoming an old, hostile woman, something she did not want to become. She figured collaborating with younger people would have to take some sacrifice on her part if she wanted to learn new ways.

# HEALER OR DEVIL?

A day and a half had passed before Frances even wanted to look at her phone. She was still processing the text from the Women's Circle and was uncertain about the whole damn thing.

Glancing at her cool blue phone as it rang, Frances wondered whether smartphone addiction was real. She had resisted an upgrade for years until her old flip phone became obsolete and she was forced to get a new one. Perhaps it was coincidence or fate that this new phone filled in that vacant space the Covid lockdown had created. It was definitely an upgrade, with access to more bullshit technology than she could imagine. She did not consent for this distance to arise, yet this pandemic had brought into existence a distance from others in her life greater than she realized.

The call coming in was from Frances's other *comadre*, Margie. When Frances saw that name pop up on the screen, she pressed the green button without hesitation. "Hey, girl! Or should I say stranger?"

On the other end of the phone, a very familiar voice said, "No kidding! How are you doing, my sister?"

"I'm good, considering the times," Frances answered. "Boy, I thought we had just about seen it all. You ready for the next episode?"

They giggled together, knowing they didn't even need language to communicate—nor did they need a cool blue phone. There was a shared space within their existence reserved just for them—a familiar spot the soul remembers as trusting, as loving, or perhaps it was a mirror that reflects and recognizes respect and integrity. They were the OG's of the neighborhood they'd grown up in and shared a blood lineage as well. Turns out they were distant cousins by marriage, and in their eyes, that made them sisters.

They were the very ones who had walked into the old Inglewood Forum back in nineteen sixty-eight to see and feel a cultural revolution take place. Both young ladies showed up in starched cotton minidresses and perfect eyeliner. They took their fashion cues at that time from Diana Ross and the Supremes—and from the impeccable style of the *pachucas* before them, their hair teased and smooth with just the right amount of hairspray. That was the evening they crossed the threshold, making a gigantic change from looking and dressing like extras on the *77 Sunset Strip* TV show to cosmic hip Janis Joplin attire. If it seemed like an overnight transition, that's because it actually was.

A week before the transition, one of their buddies from high school homeroom had stopped by on his ten-speed, wearing a red silk scarf around his neck, sporting a goatee and a brown beret. His name was Charles De la Vega. He had always been known as a cool motherfucker, and although was seen as "out there," it was his poetic language and family association that gave him a high degree of *barrio* respect. He offered them concert tickets for free. He tried to tell them about Jimi Hendrix, but instead of explaining to them, he just said, "Trust me. This cat will blow you away. I'm not bullshitting you. I have to go to my li'l sister's award ceremony. You know how that is. *Mi familia* would kill me if I'm not there. Take 'em and let me know. I'll stop by next week. You can tell me all about it."

"Jimi who?" Frances asked once he had left them

Big fat shock and awe ensued that night at the Inglewood Forum. From then on, it was flowered hip-huggers, bell-bottoms, tight ribbed T-shirts, and beads to wear instead. Makeup was thrown under the bus, and their *au natural* beauty emerged. Big daisy stickers were displayed on the '58 powder-blue Volkswagen Margie drove. Hip as shit wherever they went. Something lifted the weight of the lead pollution in the city air after that. Moccasins without rubber soles were trending. Walking around in their moccasins gave them an elevated sense of being while still somehow feeling extremely grounded.

The city seemed to open up to them as they attended concerts, festivals, and love-ins that summer. Hollywood, Westwood, East Side, South Side, North Side, and Beach Side recognized these girls as the first people of this land, with their dark hair and tans from the Southern California Sun rays that made them glow. There was power in every step they took.

Everything in the late sixties was changing so fast. Perhaps it had to do with the words of a song Frances had heard on the radio, a song about the dawning of a new age sung by a group called the 5th Dimension. There was something that felt vaguely familiar in the words about uncertainty that came with the dismantling of an era.

These two mature women had ridden that wave of change in a young and fearless age, and here they were again in a new era, facing another wave of uncertainty. This time it was a mutated molecule that was killing people by the thousands. A different kind of cultural revolution. Change was staring at them again, but this time they were elders. Both had reached the last quarter of their lives, revealing their destiny.

"Guess who died!" Margie exclaimed, drawing Frances's attention back to the present.

"Of Covid?" Frances asked.

"No, a brain tumor," Margie said, then answered her own question. "Gabriel's wife, Sally. Last week. She was still warm and he called! Asked if we could meet for coffee. Can you believe it?"

"What did you say?"

"'Give it a rest, buddy. Your family needs you now. Besides, we are going into lockdown. Everything is closing,'" Margie recounted. "Then he tells me, 'How about you make me some coffee?'"

"Wow," mused Frances. "He outlived her!"

The conversation was a solid, safe place for Frances to open up. They giggled some more as they covered more ground. It was at this juncture that Frances told her sister-woman what rabbit hole she had jumped into.

"A *qué?* Women's Circle? Oh yeah, I've heard of those," Margie said, with some hesitation.

Frances said, "Yes, I'm at a point that I'm either a *pendeja* or about to get into the flow of abundance. We will see."

"So what is it that you need from this?" Margie asked her. "Damn, girl! You are aways going down fucking rabbit holes. What are you up to now?"

"Stop! You know me," Frances chided. "I want to be part of a community online and make some money on the side. Fuck, I lost my business. I can't go face-to-face or in person anymore. This pandemic may last for years! Who knows?"

"Yeah, I get that you need the money, but explain why you are putting *your* money *in*?" Margie asked. "Are you getting something out of it besides money? Are you going to get a certificate or something?"

"No, just a global connection of women," Frances answered. "I feel so boxed in this year. It's a chance for me to expand my trust. I've met women from Ireland, Africa, Europe, and all over the States on these calls."

"So why do you have to pay for that?"

"We all pitch in for a cause," Frances answered. "Everyone comes in with a project that needs funding, and after we get to know each other, we decide who gets the funding. Our request is matched. Funding for ourselves and funding for our cause. Could be environmental causes, art projects, education for girls in developing countries, stuff like that. But first, we have to gather a circle of abundance and trust. You know, build it."

"Okay, I get it. So what is your cause, and how much do you put in?"

"Hmmm … I have a couple of dreams in mind, and we put in five hundred bucks a month and keep adding to the pot. We are also required to bring in other women to add into the pot, making it grow."

"Well, whatever you are going to do, I know you know how to take care of yourself. *Cuidate.* You know how I feel about money spent. I don't know how you make sure this isn't some kind of internet scam. I know you like all that hippy dippy shit but sometimes you just have to keep your bitch on. You know what I mean," Margie said with conviction.

Frances hesitated for a moment to reply; she was feeling the sting from the text thread the day before.

They continued to talk about all of the crazy out there. Then Margie began to tell her about an incident at a doctor's appointment. "So I'm sitting there by the window, reading my Kindle. Away from everybody, minding my own *pinche* business. I'm being considerate of everyone's space, right? Practicing that social-distancing thing. And I hear a lady at the other end of the room complaining out loud about something to the receptionist. She is screaming something about her appointment. Then this other lady opens the door and starts walking in in big, giant steps. I'm watching her, and she starts yelling about how she needs to move around and can't be seated for very long. She is walking all around the room yelling like a *loca!* Then she makes a wrong turn and starts heading my way. When she got close enough, I lowered my Kindle and my voice and looked her straight in the face and said, 'You better get the F U C K away from me. Do you understand? Not a step closer.'"

"And then what happened?" Frances roared

"She ran out the door. The other *loca* at the desk left too!"

It brought a smile to Frances's face because she could picture it so clearly. She was proud of Margie's dominance and the way a *chingona* would have to behave and take control of chaos before things got out of hand, letting the crazies know: *You want crazy? Let me show you crazy! Now get out of my face.*

It was in moments like this that she appreciated being from the *barrio* and that street wisdom that had given her boundaries. It brought some clarity to her about being a pushover for activism that lured her in with sweet language. She no longer questioned whether she had been out of place in asking what she had about Western

Union and sensing that the Women's Circle's vibe was off. She was tough enough to ask the hard questions as a means of accountability, yet she kept silent at times because she figured it was a generational thing that she didn't quite understand. The mockery she perceived from the text exchange made her feel old and out of place.

Frances felt as if she had a kind of intelligence that was hard-earned. She realized she shared this same dominant spirit she admired in her friend. That confidence and fearlessness of her youth had receded somewhat, depending on the setting she was in—but it wasn't gone. The conversation with Margie had reminded her that she could be—and was—both *kumbaya* in spirit and a *chingona*. There was a duality to her being. At the same time, she was a nurturer and had a killer instinct. She was both healer and devil. An attitude of being strong and fierce in everything she faced returned to her at that moment.

# DEEP ROOTS

Everything had its own vibe—every single thing. Time and space revealed it. Songs, animals, forest, books, land, news, ideas, names, architecture, roads—as well as every single human. The past, present, and future also had their own signature vibes. Frances's view of history's timeline stretched beyond what others could see or feel. Her borderland soul felt the rush of standing on the edge of a precipice looking west into the vast Pacific, with history to her back and possibility before her. Her memories intertwined with historical realities that somehow slipped below the radar of most Americans' comprehension.

The only boundary of her upbringing had been her own self-worth that had developed from being an activist Chicana in a family that was open-minded. Her parents were old-fashioned, and yet they were able to see that their daughter was the promise of future generations. Common culture that kept a nation glued together evaporated like sea foam on the shoreline of her own inner land-scape. Her minority viewpoint felt so rich with cuisine and culture. She was not interested in the common "American Dream" because there was too much conflict for her to digest. The history classes of her youth had been full of battles and wars in states and countries that were so far away from her existence. She had observed the way advertisements and fear of lack drove Americans to consume too much. She had questioned this common culture and decided to rebel in her own way. Designer labels were a joke to her. The thought of using her body to advertise for some factory seemed absurd.

From the time she became aware of politics, Frances had wrestled with individualism versus egalitarianism. There was a social theory that favored freedom of independent action over the collective, giving the individual permission to engage in free enterprise and the pursuit of profit. But in her book of principles, everything was connected; there was no escaping the ripples your actions created. She considered herself independent, yet knew enough to understand that everything she said and did affected something or somebody else in her environment.

Because of their emphasis on egalitarianism—the principle that all people are created equal and deserve equal opportunities and legal rights—Frances felt comfortable with the writers of the U.S. Constitution, whether or not they had intended for this principle to extend to her kind. She had lived with both of these principles—individualism and egalitarianism—her entire life and had felt that in-between place over and over again. This included that feeling of being American but not American enough because of the color of her hair, because of her skin, because of her race. Nowhere was she represented in the pop culture of the fifties and early sixties. Magazines, movies, TV shows, textbooks, and even the literature she loved to read had made little mention of her kind until recently. America was evolving, and she was grateful for that.

Freedom—the second tenet of her citizenship—was much more than a shallow cliché, Frances felt. Her belief in freedom had always had its own unique vibration, the tones harmonizing with one another, dipping, rising sideways, jive dancing, shaking her body, always in motion. Frances believed that her freedom was nothing without her mental and physical health, that her freedom was based on the belief in her own sovereignty. That freedom also meant responsibility. She had learned from the mistakes she had made in her youth—that sometimes too much freedom to do as she pleased could lead to exclusion and blindness to the feelings of the very people she loved. She had walked away from relationships and friendships because she felt like they were choking her vibe, only to realize they'd been protecting her from being careless or doing something stupid. She had discovered that freedom was a fine balance. Understanding this had helped her to upgrade her mental hardware and be more mindful of future decisions involving herself and others. Everything left an echo of its vibration, everything. She depended on these vital lessons to help navigate and sustain her soul's journey.

The threat of Covid had made her more aware of her freedom. Even before the pandemic, she had noticed many of her friends and acquaintances in the same age bracket were facing health issues. Frances felt herself aging and knew she couldn't take her health for granted. She had allowed the worry and concern of the pandemic to overshadow her habit of keeping her muscles fit. The fear of having a deadly disease slapped her sideways; Covid was everywhere now. She had read in the news that there were half a million cases in the United States alone. If she caught it too, what would it do to her cherished values of being independent and mobile? She had read that some people never fully recovered. Some people had long-term effects, and at her age, she knew she was dodging bullets. The best part of having freedom for Frances in her elder years was her mobility—to be able to come and go as she pleased without having to ask for someone's permission. The thought of being dependent was unbearable to her.

The morning after she'd spoken to Margie, Frances woke up from a deep, deep sleep with a fresh epiphany: She needed to get back in shape. She was getting soft during the pandemic, and she wasn't happy about it. She had stopped going to the gym and the yoga classes she loved. She chose to be away from people and their germs. Not her vibe. Besides, people were becoming rude about wearing masks and keeping their distance in public. Frances figured it was a waste of her time to deal with them and decided to put together a plan to exercise in the comfort of her home. Sitting in her dining room with her morning coffee, she looked around the room and thought she would have to push some furniture aside and set up a space for this. Whenever she decided to start a new project, the first thing she would ask herself was, *Can I have fun with this? If not, fuck it—I'm not doing it.* This was new; in the past, she'd felt obligated to finish what she started.

It occurred to her that she should make a new rad-ass playlist for her workout. This was something she could have fun with all day long. She could choose upbeat songs that made her feel good inside and out, songs that resonated with her sense of freedom from the past and songs that would inspire her future health. She picked up her phone from the table, opened her music app, and started picking songs from the music collection she valued so highly.

Frances's songs were worth more to her than any tangible object in her possession. They made up a library of experiences that weaved her existence, every single song pulling her into the past or pushing her into her destiny. Music conjured up an eternal flame in that soul cavity of hers.

Her house had always been filled with music since the time she'd been that little girl carefully flipping her mother's albums to side B. Her mother loved movie soundtracks from the late fifties and sixties, and Frances pretty much had them memorized before she left elementary school. Her older sister and only sibling, Lina, had oscillated between Motown and the Beatles; Frances eventually accepted the hand-me-down Beatles albums when Lina came to view them as too juvenile.

It wasn't until high school that Frances had been gripped by the radical themes of the West Coast state of mind. Jim Morrison's poetic lyrics; Jimi Hendrix's inquiry album, *Are You Experienced?*; and Janis's soulful ballads gave Frances a deep desire to listen for hours to this music that matched her own resonance of fresh and revolutionary optimism. When Led Zeppelin sang "Going to California," she had already lived it, tasted it, felt it. She was that girl with love in her eyes and flowers in her hair. She knew all about standing on that hill on the mountain of dreams. That hill was just up the street from her house; on a crystal-clear day, she could see past downtown into the wild blue West.

Concerts, parties, dances, cruising, or just hanging out in front of her friend's house after school—the airspace was always filled with music. They would open the car door, crank up the radio, and just get blown away by what the Doors, Canned Heat, or Grand Funk Railroad were singing about. It was way too much, yet it still left them wanting more. Strong vibrations that couldn't or wouldn't cease. An era of protest-conscious rock 'n roll began to shake and vibrate across the nation like the Pacific storms that roll across the mountains to the plains and create tornadoes in a faraway place. This was the music of her values. The kind that evolves and shapes a girl into a hefty kind of woman, a woman who makes no apologies for her thoughts about health, politics, pandemics, or the sustainability of the earth for that matter. This was freedom for her—and the playlist was growing one song at a time with good, solid memories.

It occurred to her at one point that several songs she'd picked had a "homie" kinda vibe, a specific *barrio* vibe that made her feel like a badass—a "don't fuck with me" vibe. It was the perfect vibe to get fit with. Her *barrio* had taught her: Respect your elders. Don't be a wimp. Value yourself and your family and friends because they are the ones who will stand tall alongside you—and they will definitely let you know when you are out of line. It was a raw honesty that supported the unwritten laws of conduct. People in the *barrio* let you know when you've hurt someone, intentionally or not. But on top of it all was the love—like they say, the *comadre*ship. A deep love for your neighbor, for your neighborhood, that always remains. Even though some, like her, moved away, that *barrio* vibe stayed alive in them.

Songs in Frances's library were living, breathing creatures. They could evoke euphoria or make her heart bleed. They had soul and extra dimensions. Her songs conjured up images of pubescent dances at Disneyland under the fireworks; hot pants and tall boots that showed off her long legs as she walked up the concrete stairs at the Greek Theater; Griffith Park love-ins on Sunday afternoons following the beat of beautiful long-haired men that transported Santana's soul vibes into cascading sounds of unity, peace, and love;

flirting with the surfer-boys at the pier before they became too full of themselves; freeways that took her to any direction and dimension she wanted, up, down, east, west, across the sizzling desert, gaining elevation into snow-covered mountains, redwood-forested groves, sand and waves, or strawberry fields forever.

By the eleventh song she picked, she was remembering when she'd chosen to stretch her physical boundaries beyond California and see what the rest of the country was like. She'd been ready to learn to exercise her discernment beyond the bounds of her provinciality. The song "Going Up the Country" by Canned Heat had her cousin Laura and her bouncing off their seats as they embarked on their journey the summer of '69. Maps existed, yet these were unexplored roads that lay ahead for Frances. This was her first solo road trip, and she thought she was in charge. She reassured Laura that this would be a fun vacation and they could camp along the way to Oregon. Frances wanted to visit a friend she had met in college. She recalled driving north on the 5 freeway; it was blazing hot, windows rolled down, and her long, wild hair contained in a bandana. Her *comadres* had thought she was crazy for wanting to do things like leave home during the apex of summer gatherings in the city. As she listened to this song, Frances, in her wise-woman era, also felt an uncomfortable vibe that reminded her of her growing pains from that same trip.

As this road trip continued, the strong vibrations of the lands and their ancient past had surprised Frances. These sensations were entirely unfamiliar to her. Her feelings shifted, and her stomach ached. Her intimate connection to her *tierra* no longer supported her once she had left the gentle folds of L.A.'s basin. That trip had proven to be a challenging one for her. Its vibe projected a vacancy that mourned the ancient forest. The emotions she felt ranged from feeling drowsy to anger and sadness.

"What the fuck?" she had yelled at one point from behind the steering wheel of the '61 Econoline van she'd borrowed from her Tío Tomás as they drove past a stretch of mountain where the forest had been clear-cut. "Could they have been that fucking stupid to mow down magnificence? Of course that's why we are some kind of industrial leader in the world!" Her cousin sat silent but nodded her head in agreement.

Frances knew that in order to make it another 100 or 200 miles to her friend's house, she would have to stop and take a break from driving. Take out some snacks and smoke some dope to settle her vibe down. Take some time with the land and cry if she had to. These new places were different—so strong that it made her feel weak in contrast. She didn't know why at first, but after several similar experiences, she began to recognize that certain places made her feel fluid. She would get a feeling that something bad had taken place there and would later find out the place had been some kind of battle site. Historic landmarks usually gave only one perspective, and it wasn't that of the indigenous women or children involved. The more she traveled and the older she got, she knew better. She knew about the atrocities that had happened all over the West, with or without a commemorative marker. She realized she could feel that cruel force of history beneath her feet. These differences in vibration began to forge her awareness of the history on her continent. It had taken her a while to connect the dots, but eventually she had. It had taken her even longer to recognize that she herself was somehow carrying this burden within her.

A new song revealed itself for her to listen to, changing the course of her memories. Adjusting her earbuds to maximize the sound, Frances embraced a deep appreciation of her origins, the kind that exposed her to respecting differences in all people. After all, wasn't it Sly and his family Stone who had sung about red ones, yellow ones, black ones, white ones, short ones, fat ones, everyday people? She remembered again her profound sense of swagger among those who did not share her beloved state of mind.

This was one of the reasons that Frances found it confusing to deal with people outside of her state. In her subsequent travels, Frances developed a sense for when people felt uncomfortable around her. Before they said anything, she could feel their vibe shift.

The first time this happened, she had been exploring the interior mountain states. Standing in front of a diorama at the local museum in Cody, Wyoming, a woman next to Frances had begun screaming; all Frances had done was take a step backward. Keeping her cool, Frances assessed the situation, then looked at the woman with raised eyebrows and sent a strong vibe of "Chill out, chick" and "What's your problem?" It occurred to Frances that the only reason the woman was screaming was because Frances's movement had scared the shit out of her. The woman had realized she was standing next to a real, breathing, red-skinned person. So in Frances's devious mind, she grinned and said silently with her eyes, "I see you. I see what the problem is now. I own it here where I walk. And don't forget it as you remember my presence. I can conjure up your ancestors and shock them for who I am now."

As a Tupac song began playing, Frances returned to that ideal place of sunshine and freedom where she could radically express herself any way, any how, with any color she desired. This place had given birth to skateboards, lowriders, hot rods, bikinis, and a fusion of fresh flavors from all around the world. Here, life was more than going through the motions of a scripted existence. Work, spend, work, spend, work was all some people knew in other parts of the country. Work, spend, *play* was where she came from. She felt the awesome vibe of her origins that gave her an awareness of radical and colorful expression. The city where she'd grown up was not a homogeneous place. So many people she knew had several different ancient cultures shining through their vibe. Some called them biracial, yet all Frances could see was an upgraded hybrid, a harbinger of hope for a promising future. In this place, no one looked at her askance when her vocabulary included words like *rad, aura, organic, stoked, shredded, awesome, órale, bitchin', ese, chakras, so fly,* and *chillin'.*

As the playlist moved onward, the songs continued to stir up the challenges of being seen as a California freak in other parts of her country. A Stevie Ray Vaughan song popped up, and Frances remembered driving off from some Christmas party in Texas, cranking up the knob on the radio and cracking up at the chaos she'd left behind. By the time she'd hit her forties, she had learned the difference between being a tourist just passing by and exchanging her California ZIP code for a Bible belt address. She'd been offered a job in Texas and had bought into what she'd heard about it being a great place to live. She was also ready for change and found herself married for the first time. It was a small and simple wedding exchanging their vows at the Dallas County Courthouse. She was a sucker for good looks, but that wasn't enough to keep her marriage together when she discovered her husband had a problem with her independence and cultural differences. Tamales for Christmas wasn't his thing. Beyond that, this taste of suburban life after living in the city proper all her life turned out to be much more than she'd bargained for, so she ended her marriage after two years.

There were clues at first; some might call these a cultural mismatch or red flags, but she saw what she wanted to see, and that was a carnival ahead. She had no idea at that time how collective guilt and religious shame work their vibe on the common ground of people.

It wasn't hard to figure out why no one would serve her at the fabric store—neither cut her fabric nor take her money at the register. She had an inkling that it might have something to do with the way she paraded dark-tanned summer skin with a short red halter top and three-inch hoop earrings. It was during her time in Texas that she fully recognized her own cultural differences and preferences.

She found her way of coping was to become just like those who judged her. It really sank in when she entered the supermarket on a Sunday and saw a sea of pinafores and dirndl skirts with appliquéd ducks before her. Crisp white starched ruffles everywhere, on huge women and small women, short women and tall women, little girls and teen girls. Shock caught her with her jaw hanging open when she glimpsed bows on their white Keds tennis shoes. Frances placed her cart near the other carts by the entrance and walked right out, asking herself, *What the hell kind of backwards place is this? Fuck!*

Frances could not help but get herself in trouble as she learned to adapt in this region of hypocrisy. Stevie Ray's song was still playing on her playlist as she recalled wearing her sassy smile when she'd arrived at one particular holiday party she'd been invited to. It wasn't long before some women huddled in a circle, giving her the snake eye and gesturing for her to grab a tray of cookies and walk around the party serving them. One of them was so irritated with Frances for not doing it that she approached her and asked if she would please make a pot of coffee. After all, Frances was just standing there idle. Frances had learned the vibe of racial undertones in this part of the country, and by then she would just grin and blink her eyelashes. She threw her black silk embroidered shawl over her shoulder and told the woman, nice and clear, "Why don't you make it yourself."

Always finding new ways to rock the boat, she had walked toward the living room and joined another conversation. It was in this particular conversation that she'd really shaken things up. A loud woman had created an audience for herself and was saying, "… aaaand my niece just came back home for the holidays. That's where I have been all day: at my sister's house. I'm listening to my niece say, 'Like, liiiike, it's like,' and I told her, 'Can't you say one sentence without saying *like*? What are they teaching you over there in San Diego? You better take some college courses that teach you to speak proper English!'"

Everyone laughed until Frances interrupted the conversation and added, "Yes, it's liiiike *y'all* is proper English." She smirked and walked away because she knew she had insulted that woman in front of her friends.

As Frances walked out of the party feeling great about speaking her mind, she heard the Texan woman comment, "Well, isn't *she* a bitch?"

It was here that culture shock had created profound resentment for her. Why give others power over her because they made her feel different? She wasn't going to play the victim, so her attitude about diversity changed in her. She would call the shots about what was acceptable to her or not. She learned how not to make friends. She got yelled at by an acquaintance for walking too slow and being too relaxed, for talking too weird, dressing too forbidden. Up until then, Frances had had no idea how many people saw her as an outsider, even though they were fellow Americans. One neighbor's narrow idea of California lay in the lyrics of a Beach Boys song. "Back to the cutest girls in the world—you don't believe that, do you?" she asked Frances incredulously. Frances was naive about racism's hidden insults until she wasn't anymore.

Fashionista, progressive, *au naturel*, confident, open-minded, emboldened, and Hollywood were terms a woman she worked with in Texas used on Frances to trigger a reaction. The funny thing was that usually Frances tended to agree with them although she knew that her co-worker was using these terms as insults because of some Bible belt belief that women and/or minorities should know their place. "Of course that's what I am. Isn't everybody?" Frances replied with sarcasm.

Frances smiled at the memory and continued daydreaming through her playlist selections. The origins that gave her so many rich memories also gave her a skip in her step as she gathered her good, her bad, and her ugly. Every song took her deeper and deeper into mental territory that brought up her delicious, mature shadows.

The songs on her playlist were three hours long now, and Frances decided that was enough for her workout and the memories that filled her space that day.

# ANCIENT

Completing the playlist sparked an awareness in Frances of missing her California, her compact family, her strong community, and her quality of life there. She made herself a sandwich and sat outside on her patio. It was a nice, crisp autumn day, and she noticed her sweater was a bit tighter than when she'd last worn it. The leaves were still green on the trees in her backyard, but she could feel change was about to come. She wondered to herself why she'd left California at all. She had wanted something different when she'd left the first time in her late twenties. Then, after her divorce in her early thirties, she wanted to run far away, never to return to her origins. The divorce had left her not only mad but heartbroken too. A cheating husband who couldn't accept her ethnic ways fooled her beliefs in marriage. Her father had asked her why she couldn't just come home; she hadn't been able to answer him because she hadn't known herself, other than to say that running away was better.

Hitting the shuffle button on her phone, Frances completely forgot about her workout. She lit a cigarette and watched her dogs eat the bread ends from the tuna sandwich she'd just finished. She wondered about being a queen as the smoke swirled around her. There was only one queen she would want to be, and that was Califa. Everything "California" was deep in her psyche now, and the songs conjured wisdom from the abyss.

She recalled that California had been named after a queen—specifically, after the island that was her queendom, according to the epic tale written in the 1500s—by a Spanish author. That was one particular version, but she decided to create her own narrative that superseded the one written down a few centuries before. After all, it was written by a man, and what did he know?

She went into her house and grabbed her journal and a pen, then returned to the patio and made herself comfortable on her lounge chair. She loved afternoons with no agenda. She began to write her story …

*The old ones say Queen Califa was stunning! To set eyes on her required one to take a deep breath and surrender to being hypnotized by her strength and aplomb. Her gait moved in half-time; it is possible that this was the key factor in that hypnosis. Or perhaps it was the dark tone of her skin that reflected an aura so bright, with rays that captured the entire spectrum of colors.*

*Queen Califa was born of royalty so ancient that they've been forgotten by many today. She and her people evolved on this island, isolated from the rest of the planet—an island referred to and mapped as being near the terrestrial paradise. It was no wonder that her beauty matched the exotic landscape. Early explorers from the far continents of Eurasia and Africa described this land as "a beautiful adultery." Gazing at the island from their ships, they saw a woman, seductive and poised.*

*In the eons of time and space, the island they call California developed into a geologic wonder. Giant granite cliffs were carved by glaciers during* the ancient ice ages of the planet. Snow-capped mountains reaching the heavens produced the sweetest of waters that cascaded into waterfalls with the appearance of bridal veils. Voluptuous peaks were the source of precious metals that flowed from within her veins. Some reported those gold and silver veins were as wide as eighty feet across. The rivers and waterfalls tumbled these precious metals into nuggets and carried them all the way to the sea. It was easy pickings for Queen Califa's metallurgists to fashion armor and breastplates for her warriors.

The flanks of the mountains were covered in ancient redwood giants. These were the wisdom keepers that watched over the changes and decisions the humans made below. The lower elevations were carpeted by red-skinned evergreen shrubs the explorers called manzanita for the miniature apples found on them. The rolling hills out to the Pacific were covered in long grasses that captured the winds and turned the hills golden in the summer months. These hills were home to another ancient tree that dotted the lands with deep, deep roots, their extended limbs providing a community for all living creatures and sharing understanding with all those who sat in their shade. The living oaks held many medicine stories for California's ancient people. Listening was all that was required.

Beasts roamed the entire Island; the settlements of Queen Califa's populace and her official residence were limited in size by the untamable wilderness beyond. The uncharted Pacific Ocean provided natural borders, within which the evolution of exotic creatures flourished. The Island was protected from the toxic pollution that was found in other civilizations. Many of the world's wildlife had become extinct because of these so-called civilized practices. But not here, where the resplendent royal hummingbirds reigned. Efficient and mythical, they navigated their way to foreign lands across the sea, only to find chaos and wars warning the Queen's seers of opening their land to others with grace and generosity.

*Somehow, many species of megafauna had found refuge in the temperate environment of the lowlands and valleys from the ravages of the last Ice Age. Giant beavers the size of bears built their dams on the rivers that flowed out of the giant forest. Packs of direwolves roamed the entire Island from its mountains to the sea. Giant ground sloths wandered about in the tropical parts of the Island. Condors with wingspans of fifteen to twenty feet cruised the skies of the upper elevations, feeding on carrion in order to keep the land pristine. Mastodon herds wandered around the soft curves of the hillsides, and the saber-tooth tigers were always close by lurking for a kill. Ancient bison crossing the grasslands would make the Island shake with their stampedes. Prehistoric camels and three-toed tapirs found refuge around freshwater lakes in the coastal lowlands.*

*This land was virgin in the way of being unsullied by Earth's other civilizations. The Queen's people had the utmost respect for those they shared their Island with because they viewed them as honored relatives.*

*The only beasts that interacted with the Queen and her army were the Gryphons. They were the winged quadrupeds that reigned supreme over all other land beasts. It was said that every part of their body was that of a lion, except their wings and head, which were those of an eagle. King of the skies and land, they offered their nobility in service to Queen Califa. As powerful and strong a warrior as she was, she also carried deep within her being a quiet grounding and calmness that was felt by all two- and four-legged relatives. She drew from an unfathomable source, and when her eyes opened wide, one could see the deep, dark brown of her pupils shift, mysterious and bewildering.*

*The Queen's inner circle of warriors was cultivated in the healing arts of this ancient culture and was led by women. It was only women who carried this tradition, due to the design of their physiology and their ability to offer to the Island their own catamenia. The Queen's ancient lineage had been able to domesticate several of these beasts long ago, and they became the steed of her army, maintained in times of peace to be brought out in times of duress.*

*The flora provided an abundance of nectar and fruits to nourish the creatures of this land. Wild rice, vegetables, nuts, and honey fed many. The seasons rotated with a rhythm that kept everyone informed of their importance to this paradise.*

*The Queen's people lived in harmony with the wilds of this land, with the innate knowledge to protect it from the outside forces that every once in a while landed upon her shores. The last invasion had brought terrible beliefs and customs that had resulted in pillage, plundering, and raping of Califa's queendom. These explorers had the pretense of civilized men, yet when they were introduced to the redwood giants, they could only think of commandeering the timber to build cities of their very own on this Island. When they saw the cornucopia of foods that grew without farmers, they couldn't help but think of what pure profit could be made by cutting it down. The beauty and stature of the dark-skinned women in the Queen's army made these men's wickedness surface. However, it was when they witnessed the size of gold nuggets in the streams, ripe for the plucking, that they lost their minds, and a fever of greed overtook their sanctimonious airs.*

*They plotted over time, concealing their intentions so as not to cause the Queen to second-guess her generosity. They manipulated her trust, asking permission to explore the lands on their own, with the stated reason that they wished to tell their homelands about the great ways of her culture. The Queen warned them of the dangers of this untamable land and its beasts, but the intruders eventually convinced her that they had explored many other continents much more vast than her Island—that they were a well-equipped military force that had traveled not only across the seas* in their armadas but over land on their horses and that they were capable of protecting themselves from harm.

The Queen was charmed by their compliments and the avowed respect of their leadership; she considered them gentlemen and granted them clearance to explore her queendom. A hidden facet of her was also activated that she chose to minimize: a knowing that their greed had revealed itself to her in their light-bodies.

So she warned them, "Do not take what is not yours. Do not harm or crush or destroy the equilibrium that exists here on this Island. Harvest only what you need to sustain your journey. You have been granted an exploratory expedition.

"Witness, gather your data, and return to your ships in one whole moon phase," she continued. "Heed this warning. What you are about to experience here will determine your fate. The land listens to every vibration your footsteps provide. Be mindful of that. She hears everything."

The Queen pointed to the full moonrise in the eastern mountains and dismissed them with a night blessing for their journey. The next day, they set out with a caravan of pack horses toward the north. The Queen's army escorted them to the solid gold gates of her queendom. This was the first time the explorers saw the entirety of her royal army and the fierce steeds on which the cavalry rode. The majestic Gryphons were saddled and bridled in exquisite tack. The explorers were awestruck, as this was like no other beast they had ever laid eyes on. These were considered mythical beings found only in the ruins of ancient lands of Mesopotamia.

Spooked, the explorers looked to their commander for confidence. Queen Califa rode her prized Gryphon around them and stopped at the closed gate. She motioned to the gatekeepers, then watched as the expedition entered the untamable realm.

Arrogance is a funny thing. The more of it one carries, the more the atomic weight of it stiffens and creates an invisible wall that induces a certain type of blindness. The leaders of the expedition ignored the Queen's warnings because they saw themselves as being superior to her savage ways. They ignored the obvious relationship that she and her people had with nature—one cultivated for eons. They discounted her quiet power of sacred knowing handed down to her from her ancestors. They only saw the island's beauty at the shallow surface of how it could make them wealthy men according to the ideas of their "civilized" world. So they chose to wreak havoc, harvest gold from the rivers, hunt the wild beasts for their fur only, cut down giant trees to build their cities, and develop their own economy. They would need to bring more tradesmen, masons, carpenters, shopkeepers, and farmers—and sell them on the idea of being wealthy too. Within a week, it was decided never to leave this place.

When they did not return at the end of the moon cycle as they had promised Queen Califa, she gathered her army and set out to find them. It was easy for her trackers to follow a path of destruction and filth connecting the campsites of the explorers. The vibration of their footsteps alerted the land and the creatures to the static interruption caused by these intruders. The land summoned the high lords, the top of the food chain, the ultimate predators, the wild Gryphons. They flew in from the higher elevations and feasted on the entire expedition party until there was calm and their bellies were full.

The explorers had found the fate the Queen had warned them about. She released her own steed and those of her cavalry to seek out any stragglers. The search party located a pocketful in a cavern on the hillside nearby. The Gryphons played a waiting game of cat and mouse and eventually acquired a taste for a newfound delicacy: wicked men. They still remembered this taste the next time California's shores seduced the ships of sailors and gave rise to their fantasies of conquering and achieving wealth without consequence.

The dogs were restless and let Frances know that it was past their dinnertime when she finished her story. She laughed at herself when she realized how fun and easy it was to retell a powerful myth from a woman's perspective. Shit, it felt like that afterglow from good sex, the kind that makes you just want to light up and puff-puff away.

# THICK SKIN AND ROBUST

Frances and a couple of her friends from up north decided to drive out for the weekend and catch some fall color. They were as tired as she was of being cooped up from the pandemic; though still mindful of Covid, they felt comfortable getting together since no one was sick. Her friend Rita had just bought a new truck and was ready to put some miles on it. Their other friend, Maddie, wanted to introduce her four-year-old daughter, Sophia, to autumn's burst of color. They packed for the outdoors—including their swimsuits because Frances knew of a wilderness hot springs along the way.

Sitting in the backseat with Sophia, Frances stared out the backseat window, musing that the view of Surprise Valley below had the appearance of an aerial perspective. Sophia turned her head toward Frances with petite fingers in her mouth and said, "You're fat."

"I'm robust, not fat," Frances replied as she realized the little girl was insulting her. Sophia must have picked this up at school because Frances knew Maddie, her mother, did not use that kind of language. Frances also considered herself an auntie to Sophia and felt it was a good time to teach her a lesson about calling people names.

Sophia tilted her head for a moment and, with one finger left in her mouth, asked, "What's robust?"

Frances knew by the curious tone of Sophia's question that she had the upper hand, and she began to recite her passion as an elder and bring things into perspective for li'l Sophia. "Listen up. Let me tell you about robust."

The little girl looked a bit confused, unsure what to make of Frances's bold language. Again, Sophia asked for clarity, drawing out this new and unfamiliar word: "What's robussst?"

A big smile spread across Frances's face. "Have you ever heard of the Mother Tree?" she asked.

The little girl's sequined slippers began to swivel in the same motion as her head to indicate, no, she had not heard of the Mother Tree.

"Okay, this is how it is. Every forest has a Mother Tree. That Mother Tree is big and tall. She is the biggest and oldest tree there. She has limbs that spread out far and wide." To illustrate, Frances lifted her arms and pressed them into the windows of the car. "Some of her limbs are as big as the trees themselves. Did you know she changes her wardrobe every season?"

"What's wardrobe?" asked Sophia.

"You know, clothing. Like the outfits you like to wear," Frances answered.

Sophia was now focused on the floral-print shirt with pearl snaps that covered Frances's large bosom.

"Sometimes she is covered in bright golden leaves." Frances waved her hand toward the road outside, where aspens trumpeted the arrival of fall on both sides of the road. "Sometimes she is decked out in pink flowers." She continued to talk with her hands by closing and opening them around her body.

As she spoke, Frances noticed Sophia's eyes moving over her face, taking in every detail: first the long, thick silver hair that moved back and forth as Frances explained to her the realities of the forest; then the bangs that kept still and touched the hairy eyebrows beneath them; then the dark brown eyes and long eyelashes, the high cheekbones that were pinker than the brown skin of her straight nose. Sophia's eyes moved downward to the lips that curved like Frances was kissing the air. The little girl looked as if she wasn't sure if she could trust what Frances was telling her but also found something compelling—something familiar like a grand ol' grandmother expressing herself.

"Annnnnd then sometimes her needles or leaves are verdant, thick and green," said Frances, rolling down the window and pointing toward the ponderosa and Jeffrey pines. "Sometimes, she puts on a furry white coat of snowflakes, and the stars above become her crown. This is the special time when her roots below the ground grow as big as her limbs above. Her roots get strong as they extend beyond the rocks and boulders underground."

This time, Frances lowered her hands and spread her fingers. "This is why she is the Mother Tree: because she reaches out to all the other trees in the dark, moist velvet underground. That's how she talks to all her children in the forest. She makes sure they are doing okay, that they are getting enough sunshine and enough vitamins—you know, growing up good. She makes sure they are healthy for all the other forest creatures to have a safe place to play, to gather, to hunt and rest too.

"The Mother Tree has all different types of life in her branches. Chipmunks crawl all over her. Birds make nests in her creases. Ants make pathways on her. Woodpeckers tap music on her.

Hummingbirds dream at night in her tiny branches. All the birds come and rest, eat, or sing. Even lizards hang out. Snakes, jaguars, eagles … Everyone loves the Mother Tree. And guess what!" Frances slowed down her language.

"What?" replied Sophia.

"She is …?" Frances began to shake her head up and down with a grin on her face. "She is …?" she said again, inviting the little girl to answer.

Awareness dawning on her face, smart Sophia shouted, "Robust!"

"That's right!"

A few minutes later, Sophia's mother parked at the trailhead, and all of them poured out of the car. As they began to gather their hiking gear, the little girl began shouting, "I see her, I see her!" as she pointed to the pine tree with the widest girth around.

# NO VOCAL CORDS

Frances felt it was only a matter of time before that minuscule virus would show up in her rural town. It had kept its distance for most of the year, remaining in the population-dense cities. She kept an ear out via the wireless buckaroo network and the collective tension she would feel when she ran errands in town. It didn't take much to detect a shift in energy—light or heavy—when she entered a public space. Nor was it hard to detect a shift in perception from those who were uncomfortable with her brown skin.

Just like the virus, the great political divide had shown itself here in her rural town. Pressure was on everyone. For the first time in Frances's life, a sitting president had made derogatory remarks about brown-skinned immigrants, calling them criminals, rapists, drug dealers. The problem for Frances, besides this malevolent language, was that many people viewed all brown people—immigrants or not—as a threat. The insecure had been given permission to make the indigenous people of this land feel unwelcome.

She had always been different and a bit eccentric but had been accepted for who she was. She knew this about herself, and it seemed to put a kick in her step when she drew attention from the pompous. She knew certain stares from others all too well, and when she discovered it, she would grow herself large and fill up the space of a restaurant—or any room, for that matter. What in the past had seemed to be benign attitudes on the spectrum of human variety had now turned into hostile stares from some of the local folk. None of this was unfamiliar to her, but it was something she had not encountered so close to home before.

It stirred something in her that made her feel rebellious and bitchy. Next time she ran errands, she decided she would try a different approach. That day came, and she was not in a very good mood. Her bills were overdue, and her prospects for income seemed flimsy. She entered her dressing room and chose loud colors to wear, assembling her outfit. She added a hand-woven textile from Guatemala to wrap around her head. She thought about the T-shirt she had on and exchanged it for a Mexican blouse with flowers embroidered across the front. She studied her appearance for a bit, looking in the mirror to make sure she did not look like a waitress from a Mexican restaurant. Even though they, too, deserved to be treated with dignity, Frances didn't want to deal with it today. She had noticed that people who agreed with the current president continued to eat at Mexican restaurants, all the while treating the people working there as if they were invisible. She wanted to be very visible on this day. She decided to throw on a couple of big, heavy stone necklaces, then added extra-large silver hoop earrings, skin-tight jeans, and a pair of high-heeled sandals she had discovered hiding in the back of her closet. She laughed to herself, wondering if she'd ever worn them before. Not her usual garb, but if anyone could pull it off, it was her.

Frances surprised herself with this getup that screamed "ethnicity" the minute she walked out the front door. She recognized that she was looking for someone to challenge her. She wanted to bait someone. She wanted someone to tell her to go back where she came from.

Entering the pet supply store with her mask on, Frances heard a woman shout from the back of the store. It wasn't the owner, with whom she'd developed a friendship over the years, but rather an unfamiliar voice. "Oh, don't you look beautiful? I love it! Your style makes me smile!"

"Hi" was all Frances could muster, and then, in a sheepish manner, looked at the stranger and said, "Thank you."

Her next errand stop was the supermarket next door. She entered and walked toward the produce department. Hardly anyone was there, and the few who were did not glance her way. As she continued down the aisles, people were keeping their distance; the recording on the intercom system kept reminding shoppers to follow pandemic protocols. She rolled her cart to the cashier, and they exchanged courtesies. The box boy asked her, "Paper or plastic?"

"Paper is fine, thank you."

When he finished packing her cart with the last bag, he turned to her and said, "I just love what you are wearing. Everything, from head to toe. I saw you when you came in, and I had to tell you."

Frances was again at a loss for words—mainly taken aback by the fact that this strawberry-blond teen from the local high school would even say two words to her. She nodded and said, "Thank you," then walked across the parking lot mumbling to herself and feeling silly at the same time. This was not her usual; rarely did she express herself this way. Her clothing was usually muted like her opinions.

Walmart was her next stop, and here she looked forward to fertile ground. She had gotten sick and tired of reading about incidents across the country in the news and on social media—of people being told to go back where they came from, of the entitled "Karens" of these times attacking people like her. Walmart however proved to be a dud that day. None of the "Karens" she had hoped for showed up. She wanted to fight anyone she could, maybe slap around and stand her ground. So it just didn't happen that day, and she returned home unfulfilled. She tried to bait someone in the public, anyone—but no one approached her. She wanted to be heard, as if her vocal cords were ready to explode into words of indignation. But it didn't happen; only silence happened.

Times had changed and warped into ugliness as far as Frances was concerned. The roots of her personal nostalgia for unity seemed weakened to the point that she wondered if it had ever existed. Men proudly wore red baseball caps with letters signifying their political stance and a different type of nostalgia in mind, the kind of nostalgia that had suppressed her kind for centuries.

Her father, a World War II veteran, had told her when she was very young that she could go anywhere in this country—anywhere, any restaurant, any theater, any public arena. As long as she could pay her bill or ticket, she could enter the front door because she was as American as anyone else in this country, he said. He had instilled in her that not only were her parents born here, but so were her grandparents and their grandparents before them. This continent and this hemisphere were the land of her ancestors. He had asked her if she understood that; as a teenager, she'd nodded yes, not fully understanding what that would mean as an adult woman and certainly not in recent times.

Frances had crossed as many international borders as there were state borders within her own country. In these travels, she discovered that the reception she got as an American citizen overseas was much more welcoming than that offered to her in her own country. Perhaps it was because she did not fit the stereotype. On foreign soil, she felt respect and a genuine interest in her. This absence of regard while exploring other states outside of California prompted her to dig deep into U.S. history so she could understand the deeper layers of prejudice. The contrast she felt was real, and it hurt. After all, she was on the land where her ancestors had evolved—these waters, these mountains, these deserts, these shorelines, this vegetation that had nurtured them. This was matched to her DNA from eons ago. Yet, she was looked upon as questionable. The pressure of the pandemic felt heavier along with the growing hostility toward her existence.

When Frances returned home, she looked around and realized she had but a few outlets for information and expression besides the worldwide web. In-person meetings and gatherings had stopped; visits with her friends had also stopped. Her world had grown smaller as the months of lockdown wore on.

It was late autumn, and a snowstorm had slipped in overnight, bringing more snow than was forecasted. She had planned to drive ninety-plus miles for a doctor's appointment, and wondered about road conditions that morning. Since she was retired, she had the luxury of staying home in storms, but this day was the exception.

She looked online for the local news, and the town's paper came up first. No mention of road conditions or school closures. All she found was some criminal update of a drug bust that had happened a week ago and an article about wild turkeys stranded in the strip mall. There were plenty of ads that got in the way. This confirmed why she did not subscribe. The local paper consisted of banal articles to make rural folk feel good about themselves. It was one of the most boring papers she had ever read.

She went onto social media and looked up the highway patrol page. There it was: Icy road conditions through the passes and bridges. Chains required! She had to cancel her appointment for testing her bone density. She poured another cup of coffee, got comfortable on her couch, and made the call. Afterward, she continued scrolling, feeling like she needed to know if the schools were closed even though it was none of her business. She cruised Facebook looking for the local paper, then found the page and typed a comment expressing her dissatisfaction: "Looked for school closures early this morning in the news. So much for public service announcements."

She continued scrolling, adding her two cents here and there. She was glad that everything was canceled, and the silence the snow brings made her even more so.

Frances noticed a number of notifications in the upper right-hand corner of her screen. Clicking to view them, she did not recognize any of the names but saw that she had ruffled a few feathers.

"Some people are never thankful for all the great news here!"

"The school district notifies parents of school closures. You should be on that list?"

"Get a life!"

"People just like to complain."

"That's what is wrong with people like you, always wanting everything served up to them on a silver platter."

"Where are you from? Must not be from here."

"The Hitching Post is not responsible for notification of school closures."

As more comments rolled in in real time, Frances chuckled to herself. Her unfinished cup of coffee had grown cold, so she went to the microwave to give it a zap. Deep down, she enjoyed the insults because it gave her something to create from, a dialogue with herself that revealed her truths even though no one could hear her. Who would listen to her anyway? It was nothing but complaints and discontent.

She was still feeling bitchy and mad from the trip to Walmart a couple of days earlier. She began to conjure up some sarcastic replies but decided to let it ride for a while. It was like she wanted to give them enough rope to reveal the small-mindedness of their opinions. The feelings of her Women's Circle experience were surfacing all over again. She decided to keep silent once again and see what would happen. She had told the truth, and that was enough.

She decided to read the international news instead, leaving the shores of her country to receive the news from England. While scrolling the headlines, she paused for one particular article. "Pig guts fly in offal fight over meat imports in Taiwan's parliament," the headline read.

The word *offal* grabbed her attention because it was unusual, so she immediately looked it up. "*Noun:* the entrails and internal organs of an animal used as food," the definition informed her, continuing with several examples: "Eating pieces of braised offal turned his stomach." "A ban on infective offals being fed to pigs." "Beef offal."

As Frances continued to read the article, she discovered to her surprise that the protesters in that faraway land were enraged due to their opposition to American pork. *Our pork?!* she thought to herself. *They love pork in that part of the world!*

As she read on, she discovered a feed additive called ractopamine had been banned in Taiwan as well as in European countries.

"Our pork is not good enough for them!" she roared, amused by the poetic justice she saw in the situation. Farm subsidies had led to a surplus of food that Americans didn't want to eat, and now other countries didn't want to eat it either. "Listen up, nobody wants chemicals in our food, nobody!" Frances said, addressing farmers as a whole. "You want subsidies to pay for your chemicals, but we are not supposed to question or oppose it. Hey, aren't subsidies socialism? Or does that only apply to children's school lunch programs and Social Security payments for seniors?" She was exhausted by the hypocrisy of elected officials in her country and the way they blamed her kind of compassionate people, as if caring about others was a bad thing. So she spoke out in the quiet of her living room, where no one could hear her—a safe place, and yet the frustration of her silence hit her again.

She was conflicted by her own sense of righteousness, yet she felt a sense of deep satisfaction when she thought about those who had made her feel uncomfortable in her own country. An organic correction had arrived, and it was called Covid; no one was immune, including the person residing in the White House. There was nowhere to hide or escape, and race did not matter. It was something she thought would have united people, but it didn't. This particular year had brought out the worst in people, including her. Her shadows that lay dormant were triggered now. The masquerade of the nation's greatness was unraveling for all to see, and her feeling of suppression grew heavy.

The majority of people in her valley had been in denial of the virus that had killed over a quarter of a million people in a matter of months. They saw the warnings of health and safety as a threat to their freedom and privilege. A tidal wave of hospitalizations was on the horizon, and death itself was knocking at everyone's door. This pandemic had the power to change everyone's life.

After the past few weeks of reading about hostility toward hospital workers because of Covid, racist incidents in the news, and being chastised by her community for criticizing their newspaper, this singular article made her feel better. It confirmed her views toward pollution in our food and that subsidizing the mass production of low-quality food would not continue to work indefinitely. There was, however, the fact that this was a very small article that most readers would skip right over because it was from a foreign news source. It didn't seem important enough to put in the national news, and that was how Frances felt herself: unimportant and small.

When she felt small, her habit was to kick her way out by thinking big. This led her to thoughts about humanity's direction. People were divided over everything she could think of: organic food, race, immigration, economics, politics, climate change, history, science, art, gender, health. It was overwhelming for her to think of where humanity was heading, and her influence felt smaller than it ever had. The weather that day may have brought in a snowstorm, but the climate was super-sensitive with regard to defending popular beliefs from something larger on the horizon. Maybe it was the Creator's plan to show the truth in everyone and everybody—the truth of our humanness, our compassion, our similarities. Her restlessness gave her a clue that great change was coming. What that was was unclear to her.

"Keep it up!" she said out loud to herself, just like her parents used to tell her when she was a cocky little girl. "Keep it up!" when she knew she was bothered by something that irritated her and she was supposed to be a good, quiet little girl, like sugar and spice. Although her parents had encouraged her to express herself, they'd also tried to teach her the boundaries and consequences of being too loud. Maybe it was during that place and time of her childhood that she'd learned to keep silent because it could get her in trouble. It could mean being sent to a corner or school office for speaking her mind. She remembered asking her history teacher why there was no mention of *she* or *her* in the textbook. The teacher could not answer; Frances saw this as a good reason not to do her homework. Instead of learning facts about history, Frances realized that she was picking up other kinds of lessons from her textbooks and teachers.

Over time, the institutional encouragement to keep quiet began to win over and wear her down. Who cared what she had to say? Older didn't mean wiser to her; it only meant that her voice was diminishing.

# TAPPING INTO THE CHTHONIC REALM

Frances mustered up her morning with a strong cup of coffee and headed to the restroom. When she returned to the kitchen, she noticed thoughts of her to-do list taking over and struggled to hold onto the details of her dream before they evaporated.

Time paused, and the dream began to inform her. She continued to make her toast, picked up her cup, and headed for the couch. She had managed to capture the vapors of her dream and sit with it.

Frances saw a two- or three-storied lodge on unfamiliar grounds. With her suitcase in tow, she entered a large room with bunk beds. There were other people in the room, and she watched them begin to claim their beds. This place felt foreign to her—reminding her of Asia because of its decor, perhaps.

This dream was so rich and vivid now that Frances left the couch and her coffee to retrieve her journal. Taking notes seemed to be important at this time. If she couldn't figure out the dream now, perhaps writing it down would help her at a later time. She was able to recall the whole dream.

People were unpacking their belongings in closets and dressers. She left the room and headed down a long hallway. She ran into a man she'd known from the law office where she'd once worked. They greeted each other and exchanged banalities. A shift of energy occurred, and she found herself much closer to her friend's body.

She began to kiss his neck. He grabbed her hand and pulled her toward the elevator. While they were waiting for the doors to open, he moved closer to the wall alongside, which consisted of planks of wood. Following the light coming through the cracks, he found a hidden door and escorted her into a Quonset hut. As far as she could see, there were sleeping quarters arranged in cubicles. Again, he grabbed her hand and led her deep into the space, looking for privacy. They passed other people, either leaving or resting.

When he found what he was looking for, he began to undress and go under the covers. She realized that she had come this far and her own fires of desire were turned up high. As she began to remove her shoes, an African woman appeared in the cubicle. The woman came in close and looked directly into Frances's face, eye to eye in this frozen moment. Moving in slow motion, Frances asked the woman cloaked in bright cotton fabrics: What did she want?

"I just want to see your face," the African woman answered. "I want to know what you really, really look like. You really are here, aren't you?" The woman took a deep bow to Frances and walked away.

Turning toward the bed she was about to climb into, Frances continued to undress herself, then slipped her naked body under the covers to engage with her lover. They began kissing, and she noticed that the energy had shifted in a new direction.

Now he appeared to be having a seizure. He was in a dead stare, and his mouth was foaming. She tried to revive him as she held his head in her arms. She cleaned him, and he recovered. She dressed him and walked him back to his quarters.

Frances wrote it all down, still confused by the symbolism in her dream. Her coffee had become cold, and her toast had lost its crunch. She felt like there was an important message for her in this dream and the timing was somehow important. It was the time between eclipses, and something shifted in her. Frances had developed a new sense of trust in interpreting her dreams. She felt an expanse within herself and a need to return to her indigenous medicine teachings for guidance toward change on the horizon that was coming her way. She knew never to dismiss the first things that came in. Instead, she welcomed the energy, as she knew there were answers there.

She studied the African woman—what she'd worn, the satchels she'd carried, her curiosity. It was as if this woman had recognized her as she'd entered the building and had come to see her up close. But why had she bowed? What did she mean when she said, "You really are here?" There was no answer.

There was a lover in the dream who had never been her lover in real life … Why had he gotten sick? Why had he become so weak in her arms? Had she been the cause?

When she wrote about the details of the African lady, she felt the energy of a sacred lady—like being in the presence of the Virgin of Guadalupe. It dawned on her that today's date was the twelfth of December—the feast day of Our Lady of Guadalupe. Had our Lady come to see her last night?.

Frances had all day to figure this thing out. When she opened that door, it led to the stories she knew too well. The story of Ixchel, the Mayan goddess who shapeshifted into a jaguar after she found out her lover did not respect her, did not honor her, and abused her with lies. She remembered the story of White Buffalo Calf Woman, who turned a young man into stone after he disobeyed her warning against looking at her with lust. She reflected on her own trail of lovers left empty because they, too, had chosen not to honor her. The arrogance of their lies was no match for her superpower of seeing lies as bright as neon signs above their heads. So she walked in another direction, away from those lovers forever.

Was this what was meant by the lover in her dream? He'd been foaming at the mouth. Was he reflecting her anger toward the men who'd lied to her in the past? In her healing path, she had really never addressed her ex-husband's infidelity or the boyfriends she had caught lying to her. She realized that she'd never really forgiven them. She'd ignored them altogether and decided that being single was better.

What had this dream been about, and why now? It caused Frances to reflect on what kind of woman she was. Could she be both nurturer and shredder, both life and death, both light and dark? Could she be …

Of course it was Coatlalopeuh/Guadalupe who had come to her! The goddess descended from Tonantzin, the Mesoamerican Mother Earth and honored grandmother. The goddess who adorns herself with a serpent skirt and a necklace of hearts and skulls. Hmmm … Was this something Frances might also wear? The goddess who walks with taloned feet, part eagle and part snake, part heaven and part earth.

This ancient pre-colonial goddess was whole and complete—until they tore away her duality. Portrayed as a squatting woman giving birth and at the same time ushering death, she was the midwife of regeneration. These were the principles of the sacred hoop of life that Frances included in her morning prayer: birth, death, and rebirth.

In renaming this goddess as Our Lady of Guadalupe, the colonizers had sanitized her image into that of a chaste woman. They had stripped her of her sexual desires, of her sullied passions and her power. Instead, she'd become an avatar of religious subjugation. The quiet woman, the unstained woman, the good little woman—never, ever stirring it up.

Frances was anything but—or so she thought. She decided to make a fresh cup of coffee, this time with a shot of tequila. There was a definite breakthrough here and a deeper understanding of who she was. It was apparent to Frances that the Lady was preparing her for some kind of change, and change could be such a bitch. She didn't know whether to celebrate or to be humble and quiet. *Fuck it! I'll be both, just like Tonantzin*—and she lifted her mug to the future!

In the following days, Frances seemed to adjust to the tumultuous events beyond the gates of her home. There was a flavor of divided politics and a pandemic out there, but it really did not touch her life. Her days and nights had become as routine as the Sun's angles across the sky. Every day seemed just like the day before. She glanced at the wall calendar in her office; the month's picture was a full moon with poppies dancing in the foreground. No plans were written down, since she had canceled her social calendar for this year and the next.

There was a realization she reached that things would get worse before they got better. Most of that year, she'd refused to travel because her intuition was amplified toward precaution. She loved to travel—but not now, knowing that ominous things were just around the corner.

In her back pocket, her blue phone vibrated. What Frances saw when she looked at the screen startled her.

Shirley: Hi Frances, I'm Rose Marie's neighbor. We met when you would come to visit her. I know she thought highly of you. I have some sad news. Rose Marie passed away last night. She hadn't been feeling well last week, and we checked in on her and decided to call the ambulance. She tested positive and had a heart attack in the hospital.

Frances: I'm so sorry to hear this. I haven't spoken to her in a while. I wish I could go back and pick up the phone or stop by.

Shirley: Don't beat yourself up. She wasn't taking any visitors. She was pretty much isolated this year. She knew she was a high risk after her diagnosis.

Frances: How about her dog?

Shirley: Munchkin passed away in April. That had an effect on her too. We are thinking of having a send-off for her at the park next Saturday. Just a small group of her friends.

Frances: Did you get tested too?

Shirley: I never went in the house, just dropped off a pot of soup at her front door. I talked to her over the phone.

Frances: Yes, let me know the details and I'll come. Thanx for reaching out.

Frances wrapped herself in a thick blanket, stepped out of the house, and sat down on the back patio. She gathered memories of her friend and felt the sadness that grief brings when a friend dies.

She pulled out a specific memory: a hike the two of them had managed to pull off when they'd first met twenty years ago, returning to the trailhead when it was already dark. That was the adventure that had bonded their trust in each other, and they'd remained friends ever since. Both were single women, Rose Marie eleven years older than Frances. In the years that followed, Frances had witnessed a decline in her friend's health due to aging.

Rose Marie had had a way of sharing elder wisdoms whenever Frances needed them. She seemed to know Frances better than Frances knew herself. Rose Marie would give her a boost of confidence when she needed it yet was also able to tell her she was being too impetuous when Frances got ahead of herself. She remembered finding it odd that her friend's favorite flower was a poppy and asking her: Why not roses like her namesake? Frances had observed red poppy motifs in her friend's house, on rugs, dishes, towels, and even the glassware. Her friend answered that the red poppies reminded her of her grandmother's garden and how much she had loved her. "My friend is gone. Such a good woman, and she is gone," Frances began to repeat to herself as she adjusted the blanket around her shoulders and watched the dogs explore the back fence.

The more she thought about her friend, the more she felt the pang of guilt for not having reached out to Rose Marie this whole year. Frances had stopped talking and visiting her friends. She felt compelled to enter a hermit's existence when the breaking news of a pandemic had come. As the news had made her aware of bar charts and the numbers of people infected, she'd battened down the hatches and shut herself in as if this was a hail-and-brimstone kind of storm. It was something huge that she had not witnessed before, yet it all seemed so familiar—an unsettling déjà vu from the depths of her soul.

Frances had been distracted by news events; these messages in her dreams pulled her back to her own reality—a reality that consisted of her own personal work. Just like she nurtured and maintained her garden, she did the same with her body, mind, and spirit. Her spiritual practices of meditating, singing with her drum, and connecting with the spirit world through journeying had all been given time out during this phase of her life. Her fears of uncertainty had overshadowed the person she loved being. She decided it was time to journey into the realm of the spirit world.

That evening, she prepared a ceremonial space for her journey into a different realm. She had a profound respect for entering the spirit realm and prepared herself as if she would be meeting royalty—not the superficial royalty of this world but the nobility of the unseen world. She never wanted to go there without offering her deepest respect. She knew that this was a place where liars and those who take without giving are shredded. Even one iota of deceit would be exposed sooner or later. From her experiences as a medicine keeper, she had seen a string of people who'd thought they could outsmart the spirit world for their own gain. Sooner or later, she would always witness their fall from grace or the loss of their gifts.

This strengthened and confirmed her ability to see lies floating around people's bodies. Even if she denied it, as she had when she was young, she knew that this was one of her superpowers. It began with the boyfriends of her youth, so elaborate in their lies, stronger at times than her developing intuition. Everyone had lies attached to their energy field; even she did. Mansplaining and gaslighting were common amongst the current political leaders of her country, and she could detect clear as a bell, even on a TV screen. She tried not to think about the ramifications that would ensue, but it made her mad that lies were hidden in plain sight.

On that evening, the drumming set on her playlist set a rhythm for her heart to fill the ceremonial space. As she entered the gates to meet her maestra, she offered her humility and gratitude. It was then that her interior landscape changed, and she found herself sitting on an atoll in the middle of the ocean. There wasn't much there, not even a tree. She felt exposed, as if one big wave could wipe her off the sandbar. Growing up near the sea had taught her to always respect its power, even if it seemed friendly and calm on hot summer days. Her mother had taught her to never turn her back to the waves. When she was a little girl, her mother had told her, "Mama Ocean doesn't want to see your bum. She would rather see your smile!"

Frances sat there with her ankles crossed and noticed the Sun descending into the horizon. Colors began to form in growing shades of orange and red. Feathers of purple clouds entered as the Sun continued its journey. She was in awe of the spectacular light show before her. It distracted her from awareness of the maestra standing behind her until she heard a whisper: "Hello, *Yaguara Azul.* Are you enjoying the skies?"

"Yes," she answered because this was her spirit name—the name she'd been reluctant to use due to a lack of self-worth. "It's divine! But it also makes me sad, like death on the horizon. I'm scared of this pandemic and what it brings to my people."

"It certainly brings death to many," the voice whispered. "It will be here for a very long time. This is just the beginning. You will see many, many sunsets taking away the dying. Pray for them to cross over, as there will be uncertainty and confusion of their ability to recognize their own deaths."

Frances began to form tears as she recalled her knowing of the impacts of pestilence on human existence. She remembered in her soul watching the suffering of smallpox spreading across the Western Hemisphere of centuries past. She glanced from an aerial view on ancient Mesoamerican cities where bodies lay on the roads as disease hovered above. She visited the Dark Ages and churches filled with the vapors of the bubonic plague. She saw ancient Asian temples where the sick and dying came for refuge from their fears.

Maestra interjected in these thoughts and said: "This isn't your first rodeo, and it won't be your last. Whether you live or die through this pandemic, know this: There is only love on the flip side of death. Only love." In the purple clouds of the red sunset, a poppy appeared to blossom.

Returning from her journey and beginning to reflect on the indigenous teachings that had provided the protocol of this sacred place, Frances lit a fire in her fireplace and poured a glass of her favorite cabernet. The nights had a chill to them, and it was her preference to sit with her two dogs close by. She rarely used this discipline of journeying into non-ordinary realms, as she preferred to walk in ordinary reality. Perhaps it was her own fear of tapping into that world and the unknowns; maybe it would be too much responsibility to receive answers. There were plenty of omens and dreams to deal with in this physical world. She had run into a bright green garden snake the other day on her patio, the red-tailed hawks were also soaring above her, and a deep feeling of earth and sky anchored her at that moment. She was still processing her dream. She realized it suggested a wound she'd been unable to see for many years, a wound of her refusal to forgive. Unforgiving those failed relationships in her life with the men who hurt her. She had worked on some of her wounds but not this particular one.

After Frances's divorce, she'd begun to walk the red road, as they say. Looking for answers to her pain, she'd immersed herself in Native American teachings. The European colonial model she'd been raised on didn't seem to be working for her at that time. She learned about intergenerational trauma, a belief that what happens in the present has a ripple effect for seven generations before and seven generations after. She worked hard to make things right in her lineage and to attend to her relatives' needs instead of focusing on her own personal stuff.

This is what had led her to become an energy healing facilitator. There, she discovered her ability to help others. The energy healing service she provided to her clients every once in a while was enough for her. There was not much effort in that, since most of her energy techniques came naturally. She was comfortable knowing she could change the world, one healing at a time. She could visit that realm if it were contained for one person at a time.

Frances was grateful to be able to witness the little miracles in her clients' lives. What they did with the medicine teachings she offered was their responsibility to make change in their perceptions and grow forward. As a facilitator, it was that moment she stepped into and out of, without entanglement in her mentees' wounds. She had learned over the years that it could be overwhelming to carry the energetic weight of it all. She found that the practice of releasing energy was just as important as the healings themselves. She realized a while back that she could only stay in the spiritual realm for short periods and needed to return to a mundane routine as her baseline. With the pandemic, the mundane had extended itself due to the necessary precautions. This was a time when she could take all the spiritual tools and teachings she'd received and use them to strengthen her own current resolve.

Frances knew that the time had come to expand the gifts she had received from her spiritual teachings. She recalled a time in her forties when she had traveled to the San Juan mountain range and embarked on a pilgrimage not only to connect with her ancestors but to follow in their footsteps. For the entire journey, she had felt watched and guided to listen, to learn, to forgive, to heal, to hope, and to gather unity. It was there on the soil, in the canyons and the rivers, the skies and the mountains, that she had entered a subliminal stratum of her awareness.

It was there that she'd been given her spiritual name by an elder of her clan. Although her spiritual name was one she had heard before, she was reluctant to use it. She wondered what it would mean to walk in those shoes. A spiritual name is not just a title or a way to identify someone. A spiritual name is sacred—sacred in how one walks the beauty way, how one walks in integrity, how one walks the talk. Frances felt the forces calling her to grow, to know her given name. Those shoes were waiting for her to kick it up a notch.

# UNCOILING

It was late that night, and although Frances knew better, she took her laptop to bed with her. In these moments that made her feel lonely, whatever showed up on her screen filled that space until she surrendered to her exhaustion.

As she scrolled, an event posting caught her attention. A nonprofit organization in Seattle was presenting a workshop called Grandmother's Teachings of Women's Ways. What caught her eye was the name Doyle Richards—a passing acquaintance she had met about eight years earlier at a Sundance ceremony in Northern California. On that occasion, he had arrived with a group of people and seemed to be the leader of them. She had heard they were a council from Washington. *Of course he would be sponsoring something like this,* she thought as she recalled an abundance of women at his campsite.

She thought about the first time she had met Doyle. He was tall and confident, a handsome Native American man who came from the Pacific Northwest. He'd been wearing two long, dark, thick braids with a tweed newspaperboy's cap. When he wasn't in his regalia during the ceremony, he dressed in regular cargo pants with a T-shirt and a brown corduroy vest. The vest had patches of power symbols she recognized: a medicine wheel, an eagle feather, mountains, and a rather large image of a bear in the center of his back. She tried not to be disrespectful, but her first impression was that the vest was a bit too Boy Scout for her taste.

Doyle struck her as conceited, but she didn't know him that well. Her friend Consuelo had been smitten by him, and that is why Frances had found herself part of his circle during that time.

The Facebook post mentioned a workshop. Frances popped open the cyber-window to find out more about it—the when, where, and how. An introduction on Zoom would be taking place in November. With her social calendar empty for the remainder of the year, attending would be possible and even easy. With the pandemic, schoolchildren and college students had been taking online classes because their schools were closed; the ready availability of online connection was one positive side effect. Frances found it interesting how technology took the reins during this time of social distancing.

As Frances read the details—the six-week online course would be followed by a trip next summer to meet the indigenous grand-mothers themselves during a Sundance ceremony on the sacred grounds of the Oglala Sioux in South Dakota—she felt a swirling tinge of excitement in her heart. Then she reached a parenthetical that made her doubts lift and her excitement grow: "Visit to Pine Ridge will be dependent on Covid testing and current status of the pandemic." She smiled as she read this; it meant the workshop's organizers were concerned for the health of the community they were visiting as well as their own participants.

This couldn't have been more important to her. It was practical and safe for her to attend. Finally, something she had been seeking for many years: direct contact with elders. Up to that point, what she had found were books written about the wisdom keepers of Native American culture. It was like an answered prayer, with no middleman interpreting the teachings. She could learn from the grandmothers (named on the poster as Grandmother Lynn and Grandmother Marie) in their own voices.

Despite the late hour, without hesitation, Frances typed the number from the Facebook post into her phone and began composing a text to express her interest. She wasn't even sure that Doyle would remember her.

> Frances: Hello Doyle, I came across your posting of Grandmother's Teachings. I would like to get more information regarding this. Registration cost. I met you years ago at a ceremony in Northern California. I am a close friend of Consuelo, who mentored me in the medicine ways.

Frances hit send, then placed her phone on the nightstand. A minute or two later, it began to vibrate. It surprised her due to the late hour. Frances lifted the phone and saw a response to the text she had just sent out. She found the timing strange, yet out of curiosity, she opened the message.

> Doyle: Yes, I remember you. How are you? Where have you been? How is Consuelo?

> Frances: I'm doing well. Consuelo is recovering from a heart attack last year. We keep in contact over the phone. She is taking it slow and easy. Thanx for your quick reply."

> Doyle: Yes, I'm actually wrapping it up here with Peggy and Terri going over things. Do you remember them from the ceremony? We got together earlier and were going over planning

for the Grandmother's Teachings. Then you texted. No coincidence, right? Do you have a moment to chat?

Frances: Now? Yes, of course.

She was surprised by her instant reply because rarely did she talk on the phone this late.

The first ring on her phone made Frances aware that she was outside her comfort zone. Late-night phone calls were reserved for close friends and family and, usually, only for some kind of emergency. The second ring pressed her more; despite her discomfort, she pushed the green button.

"Hello?"

"Hello, Frances." She recognized the deep tone of his husky voice after all those years gone by. She remembered him as a nice man, a bit of a braggart—but a lot of men were like that in her book. "I'm glad to hear from you. So you are interested in the workshop? It's going to be a great program. We have a couple of Lakota elders who want to share their stories, their wisdom, and it will help them out too."

"Will they actually be teaching the class?" asked Frances, wondering if the grandmothers would be speaking on Zoom. Frances struggled herself with the upgrades of technology and wondered how the elders would do with it.

Doyle answered her concern by saying, "Peggy and Terri are organizing everything for them. Making it easy for the ol' gals. They are new to Zoom and stuff. The gals here want to teach how to make prayer shawls and ribbon skirts and how to prep for the Sundance ceremony while the grandmothers share their stories."

"I see," said Frances. Zoom had replaced the in-person intimacy of being with people. It was how workshops were happening now that the pandemic had taken face-to-face workshops off the table. It seemed to be acceptable to her.

"We are hoping to drive a van from here in Seattle to Pine Ridge sometime next year," Doyle continued. "Let's see … You are in the north part of Nevada, right? Maybe you can meet us there? Unless you want to drive out with us. But hey, that might be out of the way for you."

"Well, I don't know," said Frances. "I haven't signed up yet."

"Ha, yeah! Right," said Doyle, then continued while Frances was trying to envision a road trip to South Dakota. "I've been working with the Lakota people for some time, you know. Well, since I saw you last time. Hey, do you still keep in contact with those people in California? I parted ways with them after their Chief Tim was so frickin' rude toward me. Do you know who I'm talking about? He didn't appreciate anything I did for them. Hell, I was the one who set up the campgrounds and brought in people to help out. They weren't even organized until we showed up. Then he made *me* out to be the bad guy."

"Yes, I do keep in contact with them," responded Frances as she thought about Tim. He had seemed nice to her, but he must have irritated Doyle for him to be saying this. "I made friends with some of the families. I know Tim Wolf. I'm sorry to hear of your experience."

"Well, that's why you have never seen me back there," said Doyle. "I won't go back after what he did. Did they ever mention me?" he asked, then continued without waiting for Frances to answer. "They probably say all kinds of things. Hey, you're not a spy, are you? Hee, hee. So, what makes you interested in the Lakota ways? You know, these teachings are way different than the coastal ways.

We are talking about Sitting Bull's people. They are no lightweights. Are you a dancer?"

Feeling a bit disoriented from the barrage of questions thrown at her, Frances took a deep breath and stood her ground. "No, I'm not a spy or a dancer."

"I've been dancing out there for years now," said Doyle, moving back into speaking about himself, as she was noticing was his habit. It had been years since she heard men speak like this, perhaps in a sports bar or something. She generally stayed away from these kinds of macho men, but she figured she was smarter than Doyle and could handle him if he got out of control. She certainly wasn't afraid of him. "I carry the *heyoka* medicine," he was saying. "Do you know what that means?"

"Yes, I'm aware of the *heyoka* medicine men," said Frances. "I'm aware of the history in that part of the country. I have much respect for Lakota Nation."

"Well, it would be great if you can join us," said Doyle, seeming to retreat in recognition of Frances's expertise. It must have been the tone in her voice or the vibration of her energy coming through the phone that had caused him to shift a bit. She knew he was an astute man, especially if he had become a *heyoka*. She hoped he would have learned a lot in eight years, as she had during that time. Sometimes medicine people spoke without language. She was reading wisdom in the space between his words and what remained unsaid; she hoped she wasn't wrong about that. "We may have to get you up to speed in preparation for the teachings. The ladies here are Sundancers, and they can show you some things. But if I recall, you are a medicine keeper? So you know stuff. We are having *inipi* ceremonies every month before we go to Pine Ridge.

If you can come, that would get you started. Do you go to sweats where you live?"

"It's been a while," responded Frances when he finally stopped speaking. "Covid."

"Oh yeah," said Doyle. "Well, the vaccine is about to come out soon, I hear. It's hard to wear a mask inside, but if it makes you feel safe, you know. Well, we were just about finished here when you texted. I've kept these ladies up long enough. We will be talking to you soon. Glad you reached out. Good night."

"Good night," Frances said, and hung up. She was surprised at how well that had gone, even though she found it hard to get a word in edgewise. She felt a strange connection to Doyle after all these years gone by. He spoke her language of being Native American, something she was missing during her isolation. She had been able to gather the information she needed and make a connection for her soul's journey. She placed her phone on the nightstand and pulled the blankets up to her ears, making herself comfortable in bed.

She turned to her side and wondered why he hadn't bothered to ask her more about Consuelo. Years ago, she had thought that they might have had a thing going on when Consuelo had mentioned he was coming to visit her after the California Sundance. Frances had never heard what had happened to him until now.

She tossed around for a bit on her bed and found herself neither here nor there. Floating around picking up the pieces, listening to the quiet evening for validation, recognizing the power of the outdoors to soothe her wounds and comfort her with its familiar vibration—always telling her she belonged, she belonged, she belonged. It was the land that soothed her, and she wondered if the voices of the Oglala grandmothers would do the same. Her mind and heart wondered about the softness and nurturing aspect that she herself needed and could innately understand.

Frances wanted to feel like she belonged—that she belonged here on the land of her ancestors. No more confusion or doubt about her. No more not being enough of this or enough of that. That being an indigenous Chicana to this continent was as solid American as you can get. She knew that she was a walking miracle by virtue of existing in an industrial world that could easily have eradicated her great-grandparents and grandparents in the name of progress.

She belonged to the next generations that survived the legislative genocide policies of the United States, of the State of California, and of local municipalities during the Gold Rush. It was a good thing for her that most of the gold hadn't been found in Southern California. She had lived through a culture that discounted her heritage and filtered it through literature written by colonial immigrants with a false narrative of superiority over the "lazy and savage" inhabitants they'd met in the chaparral of wilderness that was once Turtle Island's west coast, renamed America by those same arrogant and presumptuous people.

The fact of not being enrolled in any tribal nation of North America lent her identity a certain detachment. The stirring she was having lately was her beginning to understand the concept of being part of the American colonial diaspora, in which the Native people had been rounded up from their own homeland and confined on reservations. Frances's personal diaspora experience was more of the concrete kind, the city reservation kind—the kind her own grandparents had chosen, disguising themselves as Mexican immigrants or marrying into in order to survive in L.A. because being Native was simply not talked about. It could cost you your life or your reputation, since people still carried the weight of their ancestors' hatred for Native peoples. She saw that the rounding up of Native people was still having ripple effects hundreds of years later, spilling over into her own confusing life with unresolved questions of belonging.

Both Frances and her older sister had resisted the teachings from their own mother and grandmother because they had bought into a colonial mindset to reject all things indigenous. They were embarrassed that their mother chose to adhere to cultivating her plant medicines in the backyard and offering them to neighbors who were ill. This seemed too ethnic to them as young women. They wanted their mother to look and act like Betty Crocker, even if she was fabricated. Instead, they wanted her to be modern, trendy, and hip, like they thought of themselves. Now that her mother was gone, one of France's big regrets was that she had not taken the time to learn from her. She had passed on before Frances set out to discover her own indigenous roots.

She recalled the first time she'd gone on vacation to Mexico as a young adult. It had become apparent to her that she was not "Mexican enough" because she'd been born north of the border. Her ties to her only grandmother born in Mexico had been lost; she knew no family there. She wandered around as just another tourist. Her Spanish was pretty lousy, but before she even opened her mouth, the Mexicans just knew she wasn't one of them.

It was the same for her in the United States among the indigenous. She was not enrolled in any tribal nation, which made her unofficial. She had made jokes about having "the nose but not the number" whenever she was asked for her ID at the Native American-owned gas stations along the highways she traveled over the previous years. She was immediately recognized as a "skin" by the enrolled members of tribes, yet she had no paperwork to confirm her status.

*In between, in between, in between* was the story of her life. It seemed like she had to fight every damn step to find acceptance among her own people as well as the racists of her country. Foreigners didn't seem to have a problem with her, nor did the non-racists. They just seem to see her as a unique human. It was this attitude, among some pretty awesome people out there, that gave her the strength she had to be the woman she was. Living in between nations and cultures could be unsettling at times, and confusing, but she'd learned to live with it. Sometimes it showed up subconsciously; while walking on a sidewalk or at an airport, she would automatically move out of the way for others walking toward her, as if they belonged there and she didn't.

She rustled some more and eventually fell into a deep sleep.

# LISTENING WITH HER JAWBONE

When Frances heard the notification, she glanced at her phone and saw a text from her sister.

Lina: Hermana, call me.

Frances: I'm at a Zoom meeting. Everything alright?

Lina: When you have a minute.

Frances immediately felt something strange. She had another half hour before the meeting would end. As much as she wanted to hear pertinent information about her new online community, her heart was pulling her in another direction.

Frances felt a responsibility to listen and encourage the growth of the women she had met in this circle of cyberspace, a place she felt as a testing ground for her voice to be heard. She had mixed feelings about all the opinions going around; it seemed like these extraordinary times had made everyone hyper-opinionated.

Her isolation at home had provided Frances with a comfortable place to enter the cyber-world. All she had was time to engage, to witness and ponder what the screen delivered. Comments made on social media had become an arsenal of projections from frightened people or people locked into denial by their allegiance to some conspiracy. Rarely did she come across solid comments that reflected heartfelt sincerity. She wondered if anyone else detected these subtle differences. It seemed to her that they did not because there were just more opinions added to the soup of discontent.

Comments could go either way; some were offensive, and some were over-the-top airy-fairy. Both of these appeared to her as diversions from reality. Incidents like the Western Union conversation confirmed her opinion that the same person using "love and light" verbiage could be indifferent to the actual impact of their words. Frances had chosen to stay silent about her hurt feelings, but she also felt the burden of having to be the one to point out when the vibes being created were different from the stated intentions. At least people voicing insults and slurs were being more direct; there was no question about their intentions or where they stood. Like the guy in the White House—it was all too easy to read his insecurities in his projections. He actually stated the things he was processing in his mind—like accusing his opponent of cheating by getting a shot in the butt to enhance their stamina for 90 minutes. *Who does that?* she thought to herself. Only someone who does it themselves would know about this; it was quite obvious to her. The news provided clues to his reality every day.

What puzzled her was that so many people followed conspiracies, making a choice to be misinformed. People of authority always seemed to have the upper hand of influence; that much she understood. So she brought it back to her own reality: What about *her* opinion, *her* voice? She did not see herself on the pedestal of authority. Why would it matter what she had to say? After all, she was comfortable being a hermit and tending to her patch of land.

That was why it was important to her to engage in the creation and direction of this flowering community at her morning Zoom meeting. This past year, her choice to isolate had stirred up something deep in her being, as if the seeds of her own opinions had begun to sprout new life. She felt the struggle within as roots of her deepest feelings gained momentum in a new, fertile environment.

Frances viewed herself as rough and tough, yet she discovered her shy self because whenever she was in the spotlight of public speaking or highlighted on Zoom, she would freeze up. However, these last few months had revealed her own denial that she had projected onto others by being angry and sarcastic toward the outside world—the denial of her own voice and that it *did* matter in the quantum soup of things. Denial worked undetected in the psyche, and its power kept one from recognizing it in themselves.

"It's important to find out what we have in common and the dreams we have to make this work," one of the community members was saying as Frances tuned back in.

"Can I suggest we take a moment to write these down in the chat, and we can read them off one by one?" another member chimed in.

"Yes, this is a start. What charities are you interested in? Go ahead and list them," the leader of the community directed.

In that quiet place as an observer, Frances finally found an opportunity to make a statement. She wrote down the charity but not her reason why. "Clean Water Charities," she typed in the chat space. Gardens were her passion, but she knew that without water, they could not grow. Water was vital to all cultures.

Before Frances hit "enter," she felt the need to add her two cents. She typed: "I'd also like to hear from the group their 'whys.' Why does this circle matter to them? Can we pass the talking stick around?"

It was done. Her fear of being heard was not so bad after all, she reflected as she listened to the administrator read down the list. When she read Frances's input, she said, "Excellent idea. Would you like to start with the talking stick, Frances?"

Frances hesitated for a split second to speak as she realized she had opened her mouth. She took a breath of courage and said, "Yes, yes. First, I'd like to say thank you for inviting me to this circle. I knew it was for good causes. I felt the 'whys' would be a good glue for us, that this would be a good place to plant our seeds. I know I talk a little weird, always from a plant perspective. But that's me. That's how I understand things. It's the sacred hoop of life that I speak from." The flow of her voice surprised her, and she felt a breakthrough.

The meeting continued with vigor as the participants began to open their hearts, and sincerity had the floor. For the first time, Frances heard their heartfelt stories. The woman she resented for mocking her about Western Union sounded so much different when she said she was a breadwinner for her children and a caregiver for her parents too. She realized her voice chakra was a two-way street; it was about listening as well as voicing, and the heart was required to be open in order for it to work. When the meeting was over, Frances stepped into the kitchen to get something to hydrate herself with. She had the text from earlier tugging at her hip.

She decided to step outside and smoke her pipe. She had discovered that year that the smoke from the *Kinnek-Kinnek*, a traditional wild herbal smoking mixture, had a calming effect on the tense incoming signals of her ethereal network. She didn't actually inhale, but instead prayed with it, offering it to the Four Directions. It stabilized her by grounding her in her commitment to the principles of the Sacred Hoop and her deep trust in unity—a reminder to welcome change, growth, and letting go and to trust, taking her cues from the four seasons, the phases of the moon, and the medicine lessons these natural teachers taught her.

This quiet moment connected her with the sounds of her backyard: the quail clucking away in the sage bushes and the songs of the birds taking their turn around the bird feeder. Even the distant sound of motors in her neighborhood was part of her sanctuary. All the sounds were in harmony. This was home to her. This was as safe as safe could get.

Now having forgotten where she'd placed her phone, she searched the obvious spots. She found it in the living room and called her sister back. "Hey, girl, how you doing?"

Lina's voice crackled, "I have it! I have it!"

"Covid?" Frances asked.

"Yes, I have it. I just got out of the hospital. I'm home now, but I don't feel better."

"I could tell in your voice," Frances said, alarmed. "How long were you in the hospital?"

"A week," Lina answered. "I wasn't feeling good at the Thanksgiving party, and Sam brought me home early."

"You went out for Thanksgiving? Who was there?"

"I was sick before that," said Lina. "I think I got it because I stopped taking my water pills."

"No, you get it from somebody," Frances told her. "It's transmitted by people. Did your son get tested?"

"Yes, but he tested negative."

"Who else was there?"

"Just us."

"Who's 'us'?"

"You know, just the boys and their wives. Some of their close friends. I didn't get it from them."

Frances now heard that tone of denial in her sister's voice and decided to approach the conversation from another direction. "What hospital? What did the doctors say?"

"You know, they said I have it, and they sent me home. The swelling has gone down, but I'm still having trouble breathing. Damn diarrhea—I have it too."

The feeling Frances was having hit a critical mass as she realized they had sent her sister home to die. Lina was as high-risk as anyone could be. She was overweight, heart-diseased, diabetic, elderly, and indigenous. The hospitals in the City of Angels were at full capacity, and the doctors had made a decision to send her sister home.

"Dammit!" Frances let the exclamation slip out in her confused state.

"Are you mad at me?" Lina asked, not understanding the reason for her outburst.

"No, I'm mad at the system," said Frances.

"I'll be okay," Lina assured her. "Sam is here with me."

"Okay, I love you," Frances told her. "Please know that."

"Yes, I love you more," Lina said, and hung up.

For the rest of the night, all of the calming techniques Frances knew were no match for the fear she was feeling. The system had proven itself once again to disappoint the quiet ones who don't get heard enough, the underdogs, the minorities, the weak, the ill.

Her sister's voice was the most important to Frances, but who was listening?

Frances found herself angry again about the voices that are heard and the ones that are not.

# MARGINAL BEINGS

Doyle: Hi, you busy?

Frances: Working outside today.

Doyle: It's raining here.

Frances: What's up?

Doyle: I have some information regarding the trip.

Frances: Sure, call me.

It only took a short minute for the phone to ring as she moved toward the garden bench to sit down for a break and drink some water. "Hello?" she answered.

"So, what kind of work are you doing?" Doyle's voice came over the phone.

Frances: "Prepping my garden."

Doyle: "In the winter?"

Frances: "Yes, it's a year-round endeavor. Prepping it for next season."

Doyle: "What do you grow? I hope it's not pot? Hee hee."

Frances was not in the mood for his sense of humor. She

answered with conviction, "Food. I sell at the local farmers market in the summer."

"Oh, I see," he said with an apologetic tone to his voice. "I meant no disrespect. Well, about the Grandmother's Teachings—we are planning to drive out in April if we can gather enough funds for gas and a van rental. We have to look at lodging too. But it's going to be great for the women here in Seattle to learn and prep them for ceremony in July."

"Wait, you are confusing me. You were talking about going out in April. Is it April or July? What's in July?" asked Frances.

"Oh yeah, I thought I mentioned that our group sets up camp for the Sundance ceremony in July. Remember, like the camp we set up in Nor Cal? We have a full running kitchen, coffee at all hours—you know how we like our coffee. I always get the best roast from here. I won't drink that ground, canned stuff! We're involved in the whole thing—vision quest for the dancers, *inipi* ceremonies. I've been a *heyoka* for the Lakota for years. I'm also an elk medicine man."

"Oh, I didn't know you were Lakota," said Frances.

"I'm not," he clarified. "I'm a so-called non-recognized tribe from Idaho. That's where I grew up. I'm also a veteran, which carries a bit of weight as a warrior." Frances was a bit confused by his admission. She realized he was like her, one of the people who had fallen between the cracks of American bureaucracy. There were plenty of people who were not enrolled members of tribes; the cultural ways and stories of their parents, the foods they ate with their families—these were the only proof they had to know that they were indigenous people. She had only known people like her in Southern California, but now she knew someone from the north. It felt good to her because he was so proud of who he was.

"This is a lot different from the Sundance you went to in Nor Cal," he was saying. "Have you ever been to South Dakota? A lot different than California. You really have to watch yourself because they will try to rob you. It's hardcore poverty, like a Third World country. That's why we go in together and leave together."

"Interesting. What do you mean?" she asked, confused about his condescending tone toward the people of Lakota Nation and that he really did not have a clue of where she came from. "I spent a lot of time in developing countries."

"Oh yeah? Where? This is totally different," Doyle continued without stopping to let her answer. "There are drugs and alcohol in the rez. They know when you come from the big cities and show off. You have to be real careful with your cars, your phones. Can't be green going in."

Frances thought about what he said and wondered how different it was from the countries she had visited in her travels—Mexico, Ecuador, Nicaragua, Thailand, Indonesia, India, just to name a few. She had been exposed to the things Doyle was speaking about in the cement rez of Los Angeles. She knew people in gangs, people involved in illegal drugs and gambling, ex-cons. Some were her own relatives; one of them was her very own sister. Frances was hardly green. She walked with a certain awareness anywhere she went in the world because of it.

As she tuned back in, Doyle was still speaking. "I'm here to unify the tribes," he said. "There is a lot of work bridging the gap between non-natives and natives. I carry a vision for the people. I shared this with the Lakota elders and was trained and tested for the last seven years. They took me through the ropes, man. It was hard, but I did it. I'm doing it."

As he rambled on, it occurred to her that they had a few things very much in common: their desire to unify people and the fact that they were both marginalized people wanting to belong to an indigenous tradition. She had a desire to become more decolonized, and she felt that Doyle held the road map. She mused that this might even be the answer to her prayers. She had joined the Women's Circle on Zoom to bring people together from different parts of the world. The political division she'd witnessed in her own country had fueled her desire for unity. This was important to her. Maybe this was a way for her to explore new territory of bringing together the most opposite of people in her soul's journey. Frances liked to dream big; why not try what the heads of religions around the world had been preaching for a very long time? *Maybe, just maybe I could find a way, find the common ground that unites us,* she thought to herself.

"Yes. I'm in!" Frances impulsively replied. She wanted what he wanted. Doyle was a bit into himself, and she knew that, but she figured it was nothing that she couldn't handle. Everyone likes confidence, and Doyle's was high on that scale.

"Good!" said Doyle. "We have a few months yet to prepare, and they are about to roll out the vaccines. So that everyone is safe, you should get it. This pandemic has hit hard on the reservations. They say masks don't work, but I think it's better than nothing. "

"Yes, I plan to get a vaccine," said Frances, gently sidestepping his assumptions that he would need to convince her to do what she thought was right to protect her own health and others'. "How can I prepare? I had no idea that you were part of the summer ceremony. I've read about this ceremony and have acquaintances who are Sundancers. I have so much respect for them."

"Well, you should have," was Doyle's response to her earnest profession. Again, she heard the arrogance in his tone, and again, she chose to reserve judgment because he had what she wanted: permission to enter Pine Ridge. He was right—strangers did not just walk in without some kind of affiliation.

"They sacrifice a whole lot in their prayer dance," Doyle continued. "Our job is to support the dancers. We hold the container for them. We rise at the break of dawn to witness the Sun's rising. We stand in the arbor when they make their rounds. We pray with them, all the way to sunset. It's no vacation. We work hard, setting up tipis before the ceremony, setting up the kitchen, cooking—because meals are made for the families that go. Yeah, it's work! I'm not going to lie."

"Of course it's work." At this point, Frances would have agreed to anything that got her closer to her dream of learning the teachings and the ceremonies that were the foundation of Lakota people. Somewhere in there, she believed that Doyle's intentions had something to do with unity. "I'm pretty rugged in that way," she said.

"Okay," said Doyle, apparently satisfied with her response. "I don't know if you want to fly up here and drive in the van with us or meet us in Rapid City? But once we get the dates to travel to South Dakota for the Grandmother's Teachings—should be in April—I'd like for you to attend our meetings. Now with Zoom, it's easy for us to gather without leaving our homes. I have some other people from Santa Rosa and L.A. who are with us too. Our next meeting is coming up soon. I'll let you know."

"Well, it was good talking to you," Frances politely replied, her head spinning with all the new information she had received. "So we are talking about two trips, one in April and one in July? Just so I get it straight."

"Yes, two trips. I'll keep you in the loop! Welcome aboard," Doyle replied and hung up.

Frances noticed her phone's battery power percentage getting low and returned to her house to power it up. She entered the back door into her kitchen and decided to eat something, realizing she'd forgotten to eat breakfast and lunch. The hidden denial of the conversation Frances had had with her sister a few days ago seemed to be absorbing her energy and making her feel discombobulated. She just wanted to block it out because she didn't want to face the fact that her sister might be dying.

She explored the contents of her refrigerator, pulling out kale, açaí juice, and berries from the freezer to make a smoothie that turned out to be quick and satisfying. As she sipped, she marveled at how that conversation with Doyle had shifted the trajectory of her existence. This was huge for her. It could take her away from her worries and give her something to be hopeful for. She'd been so worried about the trajectory of external things around the world— news, pandemics, racism. This trip and the preparations for it could allow her to focus on her own growth again.

Frances had spent years reading about all things Native American. She had carefully cultivated a library for herself, considering the source of each author's education and background before picking up a book to read. These works—*Black Elk Speaks, Fools Crow, Bury My Heart at Wounded Knee,* Vine Deloria's prefaces that served as guides for reading about the lives of Sitting Bull, Tashunka Witko (Crazy Horse), Chief Joseph, and many other brave leaders—had given her a way to dive into the history of her distant relatives, making them seem less foreign to her.

Native American movies, art, jewelry, and storytelling consumed her time and attention. Her road trips consisted of finding the history of the First Peoples. At every stop, historic highway markers would disappoint her when she read "their" telling of history—always about what was built by pioneers, or pilgrims, or miners, or ranchers, or farmers, or soldiers, or anybody except the ancient ones of her continent.

Some petroglyph sites were road stops with porta-potty toilets and picnic tables, and little information was offered about the people who had carved a reflection of their soul on the cliffs or caves. No dates, no tribal affiliation, no spiritual appreciation—only speculation about a "primitive" land use by people long gone from the landscape. It made her so mad at times that whoever had been in charge of these historical markers could be so dismissive. What was etched in the stone was so very powerful to her—figures with breasts, figures with children attached, natural eroded portals in ancient ash deposits covered with carved vulvas. She could feel them there, these women who had honored themselves, honored their connection to the Great Mother, honored all their earthly relatives.

This is why she would carry a leather pouch full of her sacred tobacco in the glove compartment of her truck. It was for these places, on the back roads of her country, where she could pray and give a tobacco offering to the ancestors of her deepest gratitude. No, they were not forgotten, even if it was only her and maybe a few others out there who honored them.

Perhaps these encounters had contributed to her loneliness, Frances mused as she continued to sip her smoothie. She had found affinity with those who were marginalized, those who no longer had claim to the land or laws that favored them or to anything important in a modern world where all that really mattered was money to make and to spend.

Frances knew intuitively that what lay before her was also part of her journey to find what it all meant.

The sunset is red, once again

Is it because of the blood that is shed from the young
man who is angry or

Is it a cosmic reminder of our collective souls

How many more killings can we take

Without it affecting our sense of peace and calm

Why do we tolerate this year after year?

Why do we turn our backs to the innocent?

When they scream at us to listen, to listen, to listen

– Frances Refugio Reyes

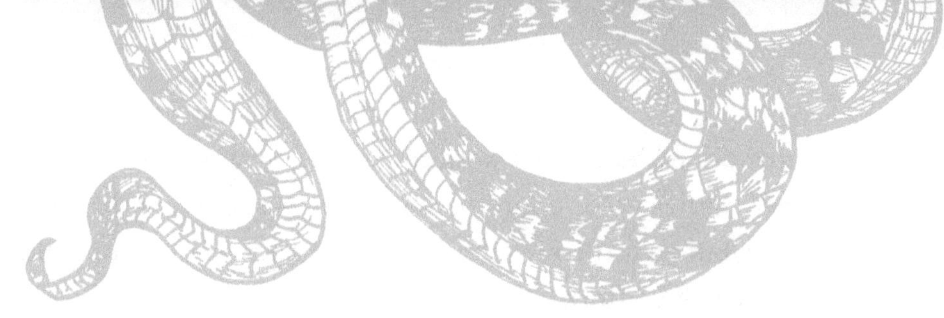

# HER VENOM IS REAL

The winds outside were howling, telling Frances that mid-December storms were on their way. Above the swirling noise, she heard the low bell tones of her phone and glanced at the screen. A *Washington Post* notification revealed another mass shooting in Colorado. This time ten. She thought back to another notification a week earlier. *Was that ten, too, or eight? What the fucking hell, I'm losing count now.*

Guns and sick-ass men. Numbness overcame her, and she continued to pursue other news. It was as if she could not escape it; it showed up in her social media too. She had to run errands that day and decided to prepare herself for that instead.

It was rare for Frances to leave her house without checking her vanity first. Her floral shirts and shit-kickers seemed to get the attention of the box boys at the grocery store lately. It had seemed odd at first when the young man had told her he loved everything she was wearing from head to toe because he didn't seem like someone likely to notice fashion. But if he noticed her, there were probably others who also noticed, so she continued to dress outrageously to get attention. A nurse at her annual physical had specifically mentioned her woven western hat, her silver arrow earrings, and her outfit's color coordination. Yikes—she felt embarrassed at first, but on further reflection, it stroked her ego that someone had noticed her efforts.

After running a few errands, Frances drove down a back alley to avoid traffic on the highway en route to her next stop. There she encountered a white truck blocking her way; the truck's driver was leaning out his window, talking to another man standing next to a bakery truck. Frances waited and then waited a bit more. Nothing was happening, so she tapped on her horn.

The truck driver looked in his rear-view mirror and lifted up a rifle, displaying it through the rear window of his cab. Then he drove off, revving up his engine and leaving a black cloud of exhaust behind him.

As she passed the delivery guy, still standing outside his truck, she saw him lift up his arm and extend his middle finger, signaling "Fuck you!" to the truck driver as he drove off.

Everyone had guns in her town, in her state, in her country. She was frustrated by what she'd just witnessed and how it was linked to this morning's news. She could feel through the ethers how angry and insecure this truck driver was. Must have something to do with his penis, she figured. Her view of manhood always had something to do with this detail.

Frances gave the delivery guy a cool nod of approval; he lifted his chin toward her in return.

She had a low regard for guns. She recalled an encounter a few years back with a male friend who had been introduced to her through her ex-husband. She had considered him a prospective lover for a second, until he'd revealed his collection. This man was a collector of guns, many of them illegal. She had sat in his living room while he revealed his arsenal. There were big guns, little guns, heavy ones, and light ones. The light ones seemed like toys to her. Maybe it was the cheap plastic on the frames. Perhaps she had thought that guns would have been made from more sophisticated material, like her iPhone.

The man had stood in the middle of the room, holding them up one by one to demonstrate their features. She knew it was his way of impressing her. She'd noticed an old glass stereo cabinet in the corner of the room full of bullet boxes. "Are the guns loaded?" she'd asked him.

"No," he'd answered. "Is that why you won't pick one up?"

"Actually, I've never held a gun in my life," she had said matter-of-factly.

"What?! You have never shot a gun?"

"That's what I said. Can't shoot one if I've never held one, right?"

She could see him puff up and play the hero; she already knew where he was going in this conversation. "Would you like to learn?" he asked. "We can go to the desert and shoot some targets this weekend," he offered.

In that moment, Frances had seen the trajectory of her thoughts and wondered if it was a wise direction to go. After all, these were instruments of killing and death. But she wanted to go there and challenge him in spite of her fears.

She had smiled and asked in a coy tone because it usually worked on macho men like Jim, "Which ones would we take?" She was leading him down a primrose path, since she knew perfectly well that he wanted to impress her with his arsenal.

"Whichever ones you like," he'd responded. "You have an

opportunity to try 'em out. What are you interested in, a pistol or a semi?"

She pointed to the largest gun on the floor and asked, "What about the recoil? I don't want to dislocate my shoulder or anything."

"Well, yes, that one would definitely have some punch to it. I would suggest you start with this one," he had said, pointing toward a lean rifle.

"Tell me, Jim, why do you have all these guns? What do you need them for?" she'd said, changing directions.

His answer had been simple: "I like guns. They are beautiful."

"Yeah, but for what purpose?" she'd continued to press. "To protect yourself? Your stuff?"

"I've always had guns," he had said. "My father gave me my first gun when I was eleven, and I've been collecting them ever since."

"So, let me get this straight. You collect them like some people collect salt and pepper shakers or Beanie Babies?"

Jim had roared in laughter. "Well, they are much more than that!"

"Really?" She'd known that she had him hook, line, and sinker, so she'd reeled him in. She was about to use a word that was a trigger word for most males, rather than outright disagreeing with him. "Is it because you are afraid?"

"Afraid? Afraid?! How could I possibly be afraid with what you see here?" He had extended his arms to cover the entire floor of his living room.

"Well, it just seems that in all the cities, all the places I've ever traveled to—and there were some sketchy places out there—I've never had a need to carry a weapon. How long have you known me?"

"A long time."

"Yeah, right. Jim, I've gotten into a van in the middle of the night in the Amazon with a stranger who promised me a ceremony. Pretty scary. I've been lost driving in the Desire projects of NOLA and asked a man for directions. That man said my life wasn't worth a plumb nickel in those parts, and I believed him. I've even gotten into taxis alone in Indonesia, only to find someone hiding under the passenger seat with a knife—and no gun to protect me."

"What did you do?" Sure enough, he'd been lured in.

"I cracked my neck back and forth and, just before I kicked the seat forward, I gave the little *pinche* an evil fuckin' eye," she'd answered. "The driver's head hit the steering wheel, and I jumped out into traffic and ran. I left my bags in there, but what the hell."

"Well, if you had a gun …" he'd conjectured.

She had stopped him right away. "No, no gun. I'm a girl. I have no need to kill anything. But I can sting like a big, mean wasp. I prefer to believe that man still lives with a warped memory of me."

She grinned as she turned the wheel on her truck onto the highway. The memory of Jim and the look on his face made her giggle. She hadn't seen much of him after that visit.

The wind continued to push insistently as Frances drove on to her next stop, the coffeehouse, and she entered the parking lot looking for a space. The lot was full, so she circled around to the overflow parking and noticed the very same big, white truck parked there with an open spot beside it. Rather than sensing danger on her radar, she chalked this up to a coincidence.

She hesitated for a moment, then decided to take the spot. She had this forbidden desire to test her fate and parked her truck as close as she could. She pretended to not see him, but she could feel him watching her. Once she locked her gear into place, she looked into her rear-view mirror and fluffed up her hair, then pulled out her red lipstick. Even though she would have to put on a mask when she went inside, this was all an act to charm him. As she tied her scarf around her neck, she continued to look out her window toward the geese in the sky. The car door opened wide with a strong gust of wind and out emerged a sexy woman. If he was going to shoot her, she wanted to make sure he knew he had killed someone robust and beautiful.

# INITIATION

*Touch me in the morning. Some quietness. Let me breathe here for a moment. Let me recoup from yesterday's dramas. Let me savor nothingness before the sun comes up.*

These were Frances's thoughts as she took the first sip of her coffee. She sat on her back porch, all wrapped up in her thick robe and beanie plus a blanket over her lap, facing east and lighting her cigarette. The dogs were relieving themselves, and steam floated around them. Bird songs were stronger in that envelope of the alpine glow. She knew that as soon as the sun made its ascent over the peaks, all hope for peace and quiet was lost.

The dogs began barking for their breakfast, and various bell tones were emerging from her phone notifying her of breaking news, messages, phone calls from other time zones, appointment reminders. Thoughts sprung up like the sprouts of spring. Although she was exhausted from winter's cold temperatures, spring's promise was just a few months away. She realized in that moment that isolation had comforted her and allowed her to explore new ways and new perspectives about her life. Her Zoom circle was going as she'd hoped; she was meeting women from all over the world. She found them so intriguing and strong. She'd begun learning and working the protocols of her prayer shawl with the Seattle group. She found it interesting that Doyle had left the group to the women but every once in a while he would pop into the Zoom meeting to say hello and make sure they were covering the basics. Everyone would laugh at his jokes and his need to control things. He laughed too.

She wondered for a moment about the vaccines that had become the latest buzzword in the news. With them came permission to return to normal, whatever that meant. What was her normal? A return to her social calendar? A return to her climate change activism? A return to her healing practice? A return to her family in El Sereno? She knew her sister was struggling, but every time they spoke, Lina would assure her she was getting better. Frances knew Lina would have no qualms about lying to avoid causing her sister to worry. A few years back, Frances had taken care of Lina after she'd been discharged from the hospital. She had made healthy meals and thrown away all the junk food in Lina's house. This had really pissed Lina off.

Frances missed her sister and felt that something was amiss. The Winter Solstice had just passed, and the days were getting longer and warmer. The seeds of her becoming were vibrating within, ready to emerge or dissolve one way or another.

The golden light reached her nose, and she knew it was time to welcome Changing Woman. She put down her coffee and gave a few strong draws on her cigarette to blow smoke in the direction of the East Wind. Frances whispered, "Welcome, welcome, my Changing Woman. Every day you remind me of your journey across this continent, changing every moment. Help me to change too. Teach me your medicine of transformation. Home of Eagle. Yesterday is not today, and I look forward to finding change today."

The story of Changing Woman had brought her to a place of understanding her own evolution—an evolution that was marching forward with the minutes of time itself. How necessary it was to change, moment to moment.

The elders say this about Estsanatlehi—Turquoise Changing Woman:

I am what spirals again and again
What can never die
I renew and regenerate myself in the sacred hoop of time
In the circle of the day
Dawn, noon, sunset, midnight
In the circle of the moon
New, waxing, full, waning
In the circle of the seasons
Spring, summer, autumn, winter

The great round
I bleed yet do not die
I keep my blood within and become wise
I dance the spiral
And keep changing

They say She, Estsanatlehi, survived the Great Flood by making her home in an abalone shell. When the flood receded, her shell became lodged in a canyon, and she climbed to the top of a sacred mountain to rest and regain her composure.

First Man, the Sun, found Her on top of this sacred mountain. What attracted His eye as He made His way across the sky was what appeared to Him as a beautiful turquoise stone. Instead, He found Her napping. The Sun provided some pollen to nourish Her and gentle rain to wake Her, yet She appeared lifeless until the song of the wind reminded Her to take a deep breath. There, She stood up and stretched Her arms, revealing Her radiant and voluptuous self.

The Sun immediately fell in love with Her genuine beauty and was called upon to honor Her. They became lovers, and She birthed beautiful twin sons: one named Monster Slayer, the other Son of Water. Monster Slayer brought about change and salvation for the next generations by freeing the world of corrupt and unscrupulous beings. Son of Water brought the sweet waters for sustaining life on Earth.

Thus began their journey across Turtle Island each and every day, She upon the Earth and He above in the sky. Estsanatlehi had a special gift. She had the ability to change form. When Estsanatlehi becomes old, She can turn around and walk east until She meets her younger self. Together, they merge to become childlike again.

The Sun paused for a moment one day and asked Estsanatlehi how She was doing. "How does it look like I'm doing?" She replied. "I have all this work to do down here, and you just float above and across the sky. Oh, and then you expect me to be fresh and glamorous when we meet tonight!"

"What happened to my sweet, delicate darling?" said the Sun.

"I'm Changing Woman, remember?" She reminded Him.

The Sun reflected on Her mood and decided to find a special place for Her, a place of respite in the afternoon, hidden deep in the western part of Turtle Island, a lush valley with hot springs and redtail hawks in the sky. This valley was perfect, as it was surrounded by four mountains—to the east, the south, the west, and the north.

When She was introduced to this fertile valley as Her hideaway, She was beyond joy. She danced in a state of euphoria upon each peak in the Four Directions. She created great gifts to share with humankind.

On the eastern mountains, She created new beginnings at that place of transformation, renewal, rejuvenation—and the soft rain clouds of Spring to sustain all life.

On the southern mountains, She created that place of growth to match the apex of the Sun's powerful rays. This was the place where plant life thrived and all creatures reached their maturity, the place where the serpent grows her new skin, that loving place of summer and joy.

On the western slopes, She created a place to harvest. Once the trees and plants completed the fruits of their labor, it was time to accept their gracious gifts. This was the place of letting go. The trees demonstrated this as they let go of their leaves. Here, the serpent would outgrow her skin and shed it when it got too tight. Here we release those things that no longer serve unity. This was the place of golden autumn.

The northern snow-covered peaks offered Changing Woman a slow and quiet dance—a place of midnight mystery, a place of winter, and a place to honor the sacredness of her origins, Her very own ancestors who had dreamed Her into being. She discovered this was a vast, dark place where She could anchor Her trust, Her dreams, and Her faith in Herself. There was room for all possibility here, the perfect place to plant the seeds of Her becoming.

When She finished Her dancing, She sat down to rest. Her original intent was to share these gifts with humankind.

Estsanatlehi noticed the sky turned bright red and looked to the west. The Sun began its descent behind the western peaks, serving as Her signal to join Him in the Pacific, to be reunited with the one She loved.

The plump of geese flew toward the river in the east, and Frances's dogs began their sun-up chase. She laughed every morning at them, knowing they could never catch the geese. They knew it too. The chase brought forth the deep tone of her joyous laughter. It would most likely be followed by a good ear-scratch. She only had two hands, but the dogs still squeezed in close to feel more of her hands on their heads.

She took another sip of her coffee and discovered it had cooled down. Before heading back into her kitchen to warm it in the microwave, she glanced back toward the mountain peak in the east, wondering if there was a lady dancing on top and if Frances might find a love of her own.

# MOLTING BEGINS

Frances was glued to the screens on both her laptop and phone. She watched and listened to each and every speech given by the senators while scrolling social media postings at the same time. Her adrenaline had kicked up a notch from witnessing the United States Capitol being looted by what looked like rednecks on steroids. *What a mess!* she thought to herself. Yet, none of this surprised her, as she had been feeling the tension of change for weeks now.

Change was what she had been privately praying for every day because she knew that tension. When change came abruptly, the tension popped like a pimple and gave her relief. She knew how to be calm in chaos and allow the storm to pass. She knew that change was necessary as movement in the sacred hoop of life. But the changes she was witnessing—the riot and insurrection in real time, the frequency of mass shootings, the pandemic, and now the impending death of her sister—were overwhelming. No wonder people were frightened of change. No wonder most settled into their complacency. Change brought uncertainty, and everyone wanted predictability.

She felt it coming, something that said, *Big change is coming for you and for all.* Frances was not able to distinguish the difference between personal change and external forces. She hoped all was well with her family and friends. She and Lina either called or texted every day, but today she had not heard from her. The riot on TV was distracting her from these worries.

The trajectory had already made its turn forward; it wasn't under her control to turn it around. She couldn't explain it—and even if she had been able to, with whom would she have shared it?

Over time and significant events in her life, she had learned to tone her voice and opinions down and live with the tension instead. This ability to feel chaos and pandemonium before they happened had been with her for most of her lifetime. Sometimes she just wanted to shout out like a little chicken, "The sky is falling!" and warn others that something ominous was coming. Of course, she never knew what that was exactly. How could she describe something that had not yet occurred without knowing what it looked like? She had learned to live with a personal antenna that was much louder than her public comments.

It had begun when she was a young girl and had tried to explain the spirits she'd seen in her backyard beneath the camellia bushes or hanging around the bougainvillea arbor. Nature spirits were aware of her as she was aware of them. Her mother had been courteous as Frances had explained them to her, not asking too much but, at the same time, welcoming her little girl's vivid relationship to the earth. It wasn't until Frances had walked into a larger world beyond the confines of her home space that she'd faced questions about her ability to see beyond the veil. Some people would respond by mocking her, and it was very clear to her that she was being made fun of.

This way of seeing never left her, but her way of expressing it changed. This particular pressure wave she was witnessing in real time on her TV was all too familiar. The first time she'd felt collective tension had been during the sixties. On a stifling hot Southern California day, she had felt a certain wobble roll through her yard. A few hours later, the sky had turned black, and the tension had grown thicker. She'd run into the house and found her mother crying in front of the TV cabinet. Watts was burning down.

Like that hot summer of tension, it was now the cold winter of uncertainty Frances observed as she continued to watch the mayhem on live news. It felt familiar, yet her eyes had to adjust to the homogenized texture of the people rioting. A motley crew of discontents and zealots. What was unfamiliar this time was that the disenfranchised were white folk. *How can that be?* she wondered.

For decades, she had not only witnessed but participated in the protest of America. The East L.A. walkouts, the Vietnam protest, women's rights, unionizing of farm workers, Alcatraz, Black Panther marches, and whatever else caused a stir in the system. But it had always been a thing of being a minority voice, the underdog—of reaching out for social justice in a country that promised equality. What was this insurrection about? The system of laws had always favored these rioters at the Capitol. Were they defending a lie they were told about the election—that their guy had actually won in spite of not being declared the winner? Or was it that they couldn't handle the truth, so they were about to string up the vice president for it? It was all so crazy to her.

Maybe this was the great change she felt. So-called truth and justice for all were being exposed as false. The house of cards was tumbling down, revealing those concepts to be mere illusions, tired of being used by so-called patriots. A hard truth was there for all to see as the hypocrisy of the president's followers had been exposed by their savage behavior.

Frances had also witnessed that with chaos, change was inevitable. Change could be gentle, or it could cause revolutions. Change was necessary for new growth, for letting go of the old and trusting the process of it all.

These events forged a seed in her soul, and that seed helped her to grow a sense of her own sovereignty, independent of the script the system was trying to force-feed her. She remembered the changes that had followed other tension periods and found that place of trust in herself again.

Through the cold night, Frances continued to watch and listen to America's accumulation of wounds, a festering form of discharge oozing out of the heart chamber of her nation. The womb of the Capitol was being raped before her eyes. No wonder the impending feeling she had been living with was strong—stronger than any other time in her life. If these people were successful tonight, it could perhaps mean that the horrors of white supremacy would follow. She was watching a sort of cannibalism of people destroying their own kind—the very people who were never excluded from their rights to own guns and just went ahead and bought more, the people who were never excluded from their beliefs and just built more stadiums into megachurches. The very people who were given superior educations and access to white-collar jobs had just used their credit cards to purchase airline tickets and stay in exclusive Washington, D.C., hotels so they could riot in protest of an election that was lost to them.

It was late, and Frances heard her phone ringing in the living room. Once again, she thought of how she never liked late-night calls because they implied some kind of emergency. After watching the news, she just wasn't in the mood to deal with anything. She reluctantly answered it. It was her nephew, Sam. "Nina?" He was also her godson, so he addressed her in the way all Chicanos address their godmothers to express love and respect. She was his aunt, but his mom had taught him early on to call her *Nina*.

"Yes, what's up?" said Frances.

She heard Sam's voice say, "My mom has passed."

"What?! Where is she?" Frances responded, frantic.

"Here at the hospital," he said. "We brought her back today when she said she wasn't feeling good. She didn't make it through the night."

Frances held the phone next to her heart, feeling that the change she had been yearning for had come but not in the way she had hoped. She raised the phone to her ear again and told her nephew, "I'll leave as soon as I can."

"We got this, Nina," said Sam. "Let us take care of it. We are men now. I want to make my mom proud. I'll keep you in the loop when we get more information."

"What about arrangements? Money?" asked Frances.

"The Brotherhood is taking care of her," said Sam. "That's what she told me last week. She was having a hard time last week, but you know she always comes out of it. Since she has had that Covid, she was in and out of the hospital."

"Why didn't you tell me?"

"Ah, you know my mom. She didn't want anyone to know. Kept saying she was alright."

"I can't … I can't …" Frances tried to reply, but she felt her heart had swallowed her head.

"Nina, please take care of yourself. You know that I love you."

"Yes. I love you too."

Change had come. She just hadn't realized how close to home it would be for her.

# THRESHOLD OF CHANGE

Frances packed her hefty truck the night before leaving for the funeral. As she lifted her suitcase into the cab, she looked up and caught wet snowflakes on her face. This storm would delay her trip by making it a two-day drive. She knew she could plow right through as long as she arrived before noon on Saturday.

The next morning, she could see a glow illuminating the ground, even before she pulled back the curtains to find that four inches of snow covered her backyard. Mentally, she kicked into four-wheel drive as her truck would do in an hour or so. She gathered her computer and toiletries into the last bag, picked up her travel mug full of coffee, and then started up the engine.

By the time she made her way to the highway, the asphalt was wet but not covered like the roads leading to it had been. This driving day would be a wonder.

No one else was on the road as she climbed the summit. Steam rose from the lanes ahead of her, causing clouds to drift upward into swirls of snow. A kind of tunnel vision kept her mesmerized while she listened to the songs on her playlist. Songs that had chiseled her personality. Songs she had experienced live with her sister many years ago.

She held a steady course, following the broken lines painted on the road and knowing that a flood was welling up inside of her. Finally, when she felt the image of her older sister's smile, the dam burst. She wanted to pull over but could not find a safe spot to do so. She grabbed a paper towel, wiped her face, and cried some more.

Nothing could stop Frances from reaching her destination today—just like her sister's devotion whenever Frances had found herself in trouble. Lina had been able to find her anywhere in the City of Angels. GPS hadn't existed in those days. Lina would show up anywhere—any address, any jail, any protest, any party—to rescue her younger sister. Frances remembered the relief she would feel at the sound of her sister's idling sixty-eight Camaro engine. Lina would shift her gears in neutral and slowly step on the gas pedal until it made contact with the floor, increasing the sound of the modified glasspacks on the Camaro's exhaust system so that everyone in the vicinity would know she had arrived. It was a California thing amongst the lowriders and the hot rods.

In that white moment of solace while driving, Frances realized all she had taken for granted. Lina had been a guardian of epic proportions. She had been larger than life, a true warrior woman. What had shifted for Frances was that this was the first time in her life she felt vulnerable. Her parents had passed away years ago, and now her guardian was gone. Frances's back felt exposed. Lina had always been there for her.

The matrilineal origins of these sisters were on Catalina Island, where their mother had been born. Their mother was about the only thing they had in common as they developed into women. One sister, a *chola,* and the other, an ol' hippy. Their mother knew the medicine ways of indigenous plants and foods, and the girls sometimes felt shame when she was called to help and to heal. Their mother was the neighborhood *curandera,* and it made them appear different in the neighborhood. If a child had an upset stomach or constipation or a fever perhaps, Esperanza would deliver. She could often be seen carrying a teapot wrapped in a towel, walking down the street to a neighbor's house dressed in a modest calico frock and wearing a cap, a long wool sweater or a shawl draped over her shoulders.

This was certainly not the way the more modern mothers of the sixties dressed on their avenue. Most of the neighbors got their hairdos from a lady down the street who had converted her laundry room into a beauty shop. The mothers took their fashion cues from the magazines and television shows of the time. Betty Crocker was all the rage, and Esperanza did not seem to fit that mold, nor want to.

Young women naturally rebel, but these sisters took it to a new level. Lina began to wear eyeliner that reached her temples and tease her hair into smooth beehives. She had a natural creative side that allowed her to experiment with combs, dyes, and lacquer. She would spend hours in front of her bureau mirror while Frances leaned on her elbows at the far end. Lina would warn her to back up, but she didn't care and would inhale the chemical vapors anyway.

Frances would see her sister transform into a Hollywood star and walk out the door telling their parents that she was going to the show. Frances knew that wasn't where her sister was going; Lina's friends would pick her up for some forbidden teenage adventure. Frances would wait up until Lina snuck back into their bedroom past her curfew. As Lina peeled off her clothing and dropped it on the floor, Frances would detect the foul mixture of odors like tobacco and alcohol.

"Hey, go to sleep," Lina had told her when she noticed Frances awake on one of these nights.

"Why should I?" Frances had answered defiantly.

"Because you're a brat."

"Did you have sex?" Frances had asked boldly.

"Ohhh," Lina had said, a little shocked. "What do you know about that?"

"I heard it makes your boobs grow, and yours are getting bigger," Frances had answered.

Lina had thrown her pillow in the dark toward her sister's voice. "Mind your own boobs! You have some growing too! Ha, pretty soon Mom is going to have to take you to JCPenney for a training bra!"

"Shut up!" Frances had protested.

But Lina had the last word: "Now, go to sleep! Brat!"

Laughing through her tears at this memory, Frances finally found a turnout and pulled off of the highway. It was a viewing point on a precipice with a silver-green lake below. Clouds floated just beneath her as she stepped out of her truck.

It was divine timing—she knew this as she stretched out her legs and took a breather. What a deep breath it was! The silence of snow and no traffic on the road made it even deeper. She wanted to cry more but found that she couldn't, so she stopped trying and just enjoyed the specular view of new Earth forming from the remnants of young volcanoes in the middle of an ancient lake.

Feeling the calm that surrounded her, Frances climbed back into her truck. She started up her engine and began her descent from elevation across the Sierras into the Mojave Desert, to that place she had once called home. While driving down the grade, she wasn't surprised that the first song that popped up on her playlist was "Little Wing." It felt like she was flying with a very appropriate soundtrack of lyrics about butterflies and zebras, moonbeams and fairytales, walking through the clouds. She could feel that her sister was without pain and was now her guardian angel.

The next day, as she reached her destination, Frances pulled into the parking lot and wondered if this was the right place. There were just two other cars parked next to an unimaginative one-story building.

Before searching for answers, she decided to light a cigarette and contemplate her next move. She saw a concrete bench next to a broken pond in the shade of the building and decided to get out into the Southern California heat. She grabbed her keys and used her carabiner to attach them to her belt loop—a lesson her now-deceased sister had taught her. She could hear her words in a silent whisper: "Always keep your tank full and carry your keys on you in case you have to bolt."

Frances felt her city vibe kick in and remembered to lock her door, even though she was just going to sit fifty feet away in plain sight. Due to living in a rural community, she was out of practice with this habit. The sun's rays felt thick and penetrating as they bounced off the black asphalt. This was more heat than she was accustomed to, having just left winter conditions up north.

She was gathering her thoughts in the swirling vapor of tobacco when she recognized Jimmy behind his mask. He was a very old friend—her sister's ex-boyfriend, in fact. Seeing him walk toward her gave her a clue that she was at the right place and didn't need to resort to texting her nephews. She was here. Her sister was inside, and she could feel her.

"Hey, it's been a while," he said. "My condolences, Frances. You're still looking great. You don't change." Jimmy, the man in front of her, had not changed much, either. His full head of hair was still there, but now, graceful shades of silver highlighted his face. She could see the subtle wrinkles of his skin. He had always been a sharp dresser, and she glanced at his polished black shoes and the stiff crease on his slacks. He took off his mask and said, "I think I'll join you if you don't mind," as he pulled out his own pack of cigarettes.

Frances smiled and reached out for a hug. "You don't change, either. I could recognize you, mask or not. How you doing?"

"A little awkward, you know. I came early." He seemed uncomfortable.

"Yes, I told the boys I would meet them here. I wasn't sure if I was in the right place until I saw you. Like ol' times, you were always there for her—and me too."

"Hey, you know, we are all relatives, after all. Do you want to go inside before everyone gets here?"

"In a minute," she responded.

"Yeah, sure. Never see you around anymore. How is it living up there? How long has it been since you left the neighborhood?"

Frances took a couple of drags before returning to the conversation. She remembered the tall, lean, dark-skinned boy who had hung around her house for years, courting her sister. He had become an extra set of eyes in her sister's protection posse. Frances had gone to a ditching party, where a couple of her high-school girlfriends had thought it was worth it to cut their classes during school hours because they had heard some of the good-looking dudes from the neighborhood were going to be there. Jimmy had walked in, and it hadn't been long before she'd heard her sister revving up her engine in front of the house and realized she was busted. "Oh yeah, it's been years."

The minute she stepped into the lobby, she could feel her heart sink into a void that was seldom revealed. It was a different kind of resistance that created liquid walls and collapsing vulnerabilities all at the same time. She felt Jimmy taking steps right behind her, close enough to catch her if she fell down. She stopped because she had to and stood in the back of the chapel, her vision zeroing in on the lavender enameled urn.

The flood of thoughts began to descend into the void and fill her with questions. Her first thought was, *How could she fit in there?* Lina had been larger than life. All that was left of her buxom brunette sister, there in that jar. *Why wasn't I there for her? Why didn't she tell me she was in pain? I should have, could have, would have.*

Instead of walking forward, she decided to sit in the last pew. Without words, Jimmy assisted her and took a seat next to her. As they sat in silence, the chapel remained empty for some time. Gravity seemed to keep her seated until she heard the voice of her nephew. "Nina!"

"Sam." Frances turned toward the entrance of the chapel and reached out to hug her nephew.

"Yeah, she's gone now."

"I'm so sorry. I know how much she loved you."

"She loved you too."

Frances mumbled, "I didn't realize how sick she was."

"Ah, Nina, this Covid thing was hard on her. She just wanted to be home with her pets. She didn't want to see the doctors or be in a hospital. You know my mom."

Frances shifted into herself once again and said, "Stubborn, you mean?"

He smiled at her and nodded in agreement. "Why don't you come up and sit with us?" he offered.

"No, I'm good right here. Is that okay?"

"Sure, it's okay."

She remained seated, and as people walked by, she began to recognize faces from her past. Jimmy excused himself, whispering, "If you need me, I'll be close by."

Frances nodded to let him know she was okay. People were walking past her in the main aisle and slipping into the pews up front. A preacher appeared at the podium and began to introduce himself as a follower of Jesus and share his bona fides of being holy. The preacher told of the glory of celebrating one's life through Jesus and only Jesus, how the only way to heaven was through belief in Jesus.

By this time, Frances knew that this fool knew nothing about her sister and was up there just babbling on. She figured the mortuary had arranged this as the protocol for all funerals, and the masses just swallowed it as good.

After a few minutes, Frances wondered: Did he even know the name her sister went by? This preacher kept referring to Catalina, but nobody called her that. It was always Lina. The more the preacher talked, the more he looked like a *pendejo* to Frances. Her sister had been anything but a religious fanatic.

A group of hard-looking men, all dressed alike, entered the row of pews just in front of her and next to her. Their presence made a statement of super-thick machismo, the kind she had not seen much of since retreating into her own private bubble. They were polite in asking her to make room for more on her row, and she quietly slid toward the wall. She suddenly found herself surrounded and didn't know if she should be concerned for her safety. There was a shift in the energy field around her; it felt dangerous, yet she simply sat in silence and absorbed it as real.

In order to adjust to this testosterone charge, she began to focus on the symbols embroidered on the back of their leather vests. She did not know any of these men—not one of them. They reminded her of the split in lifestyle between her sister and herself that had taken place when Frances had decided to move up north, away from the city—how her sister had become involved in the underbelly of the city's hierarchy. Lina had become a driver, picking up or dropping off things that Frances did not want to know anything about. They each had been ambitious in their own flavor of power. Frances had forged ahead in academia, while her sister had forged ahead in a motorcycle brotherhood. It didn't matter how different the sisters had become; Chicanas were like glue, especially sisters. They were always there for each other *con mucho respeto.*

By this time, Frances had lost interest in the preacher's sermon. She figured her sister had something to do with her current predicament. Lina must be cracking up. Frances could hear what she would be saying: "See? You should have gotten your ass up when Sam told you to sit up front! Now look at you! Ha!" The man next to her heard Frances laugh to herself and gave her a sideways glance.

After announcing to the guests that their remembrances of Lina were now welcome, the preacher finally shut up for a moment. A man Frances recognized as their childhood neighbor walked up to the podium and began to cry as he spoke about "Lina." Frances sighed with relief that her sister's official *barrio* name was finally being used.

When the neighbor was finished speaking, another lady got up and told of her memories working with Lina. Frances recognized her sister's friend as the supervisor at the company where she had worked. Her sister had made good money there.

The preacher interjected and took hold of the microphone again, proclaiming how he continued to harbor refuge in Jesus, followed with threats of guilt for not attending church on Sundays. Frances hit her limit, and her temper began to peak as she thought to herself, *Enough with the Christian drivel.*

Words fell out of her mouth as she said out loud, "Gimme a fuckin' break. Lina never spent a day in church!" The men surrounding her extended their necks, turning toward her and breaking out in a controlled chortle. The preacher held the good book in the air and seemed to be on a roll.

Frances couldn't take another word and stood up. Without hesitation, she managed to carefully step across the boots of the man sitting next to her. When the rest of the men noticed her force coming down the row, they either got up or slid out of the pew to make room.

The preacher seemed surprised to see Frances walking directly toward him as he continued speaking into the microphone. He lowered his book on the podium, gesturing to inquire: What was she doing?

"Excuse me," she said. "May I say a word?"

"Well, I'm … Of course. Please," he said, stepping aside.

Frances turned toward him and said, "Thank you. Why don't you have a seat now?" She pointed to a space in the front pew. The preacher looked annoyed at Frances as an emboldened woman but could see by the faces of the audience that Frances was someone familiar who carried some weight.

Although she was nervous speaking in public, her anger overrode her insecurity at that moment. The thought of someone leading this service without knowing one iota of her big sister's distinctive character infuriated her to no end. This was not proper, not in alignment with who Lina was.

Frances closed her eyes and stood in silence for a moment to ground herself. When she opened them, the first thing she saw was her nephews and their wives sitting directly in front of her. She could see that the room was filled with masked people but did not look directly at any of them. She gave the preacher a sideways glance, as if subconsciously telling him: *Relax because you are going to be sitting down for a while.* She felt shaky inside.

Tears began to well up as she offered her condolences and told the boys how much their mother had loved them. "She would do anything for you, as she would do for me too."

Frances went silent, as she did not know what to say next. Then a flush in her cheeks prompted her to go on because her heart needed to speak. "Do you know that she never said no to me? Not once. When I would get myself into trouble, all I would have to do is call her. She would show up in any part of this city. She drove it like it belonged to her. Every street—it was all hers. Maybe it had to do with our ancestors, the first people of Los Angeles. Our mother was Chumash or Tongva—we don't know—but we know we are indigenous here. I feel it's appropriate to give acknowledgement to our ancestors of this land. Thank you for hosting us here. We call upon you to meet our Lina on the other side. I call upon the sacred space of the Four Directions—east, south, west, and north—to help us navigate this moment of love and respect for our departed sister. I call upon Mother Earth and her gifts to all of us. I call upon Great Spirit and our love and gratitude for each other in this lifetime."

Frances could feel the preacher's shock and threw him an even stronger side-eye while she continued to speak. "If you knew her *like we know her*"—this time, Frances looked directly at the preacher—"you know she would give the shirt off her back to make sure you were covered. She made sure everyone was okay, like a big mama bear. No one fucked with her cubs, with her *gente*."

The preacher didn't laugh, but the guests did. Frances continued: "She was my guardian—something I took for granted until I found out how much she covered my back. One day after school, there was a rowdy chick who was going to kick my ass for defending my schoolmate. I was talking big like I wanted to fight. It didn't happen, but the next day, my sister asked, 'How was school?'

"'Good,' I told her.

"'Oh yeah? Anything happen?'

"'No,' I said.

"'Oh really? No one apologized to you?'

"I realized my sister knew what had happened because the girl that was going to kick my ass had approached me in the library and said everything was cool. It had surprised me.

"My sister revealed that the good ol' tamale wireless let her know that I was in trouble. That gossip chain worked faster than any social media did, ha! In fact, it was around way before smartphones.

I found out that she drove over to the chick's house after work and threatened her. The chick counter-threatened Lina and said she would get *her* older sister to kick Lina's ass. Lina let the chick know that she knew her older sister well, and if she touched one fuckin' hair on me, she would kick not only the chick's ass but the chick's sister's ass and the chick's mother's ass too. In fact, if this certain chick did not apologize to me the next day, she would be coming after her!

"This is what I mean. She was an example of everything I wanted to be: fierce, beautiful, strong, aware, cool, sexy, smart. She took me everywhere. Took me to work with her at the playground, taught me how to swim, taught me to drive stick shift, taught me to wear make-up and look groovy. She taught me how to survive and thrive in our hood.

"Because of her, I became a strong, independent woman. I carry what I learned from her everywhere I have lived, everywhere I travel on this Earth. She taught me so many things but mostly to value my life—to value life itself, to value the lives of your family, of your friends, of your pets. To value the important things—and always, always keep your bitch on!"

She was approaching the end of her tribute. "Sister," she said out loud, "I know you have the keys to that golden super-sport Camaro of yours as you shift into high gear in the heavenly realm!" Frances took a deep breath and wiped the tears from her eyes as those who had also loved her sister laughed along from the pews.

# SWALLOWED BY THE SERPENT

Frances had stayed in L.A. with her *comadre* Margie for a few months following the funeral. They drove each other crazy but had enough mutual respect to give each other space when it was needed. Frances wanted to be at home but also felt obligated to tend to her sister's unfinished business. While there, she attended a celebration of life where her sister's homies played oldies and barbecued a ton of meat. The yard was full of black leather vests and riding boots. This gang was notorious for their violence, yet when they were on this mission to see one of their own cross over, their brotherhood shined. It was a foreign world for Frances, the epitome of what she despised: the ultra-toxic masculine machine that threatened the world with violence, drugs, and crime. She saw it as no different from the war machines of the world. The only difference was that taxes paid for those wars.

It had always been difficult for Frances to understand her sister's choice to ride this road. Yet, what Frances witnessed this day from the homies was total respect and love for her sister. It made her accept a different reality, that her sister could exist and thrive in a hard-core, macho world and be respected as a woman. Frances had been resisting and rebelling against this type of patriarchy for years, only to discover that her sister had found a place in it. It was all about having respect, no matter where your choices directed you. That respect began with self, and Lina had plenty of it. Frances was beginning to change her perspective toward her sister's friends, even though it was a struggle because it meant deconstructing her beliefs in the midst of her grief.

Then there was the clean-up of her sister's house and all the shit Lina had accumulated. Lina's sons had shown up, and after the first day, they'd decided they really didn't want anything from their mother's home. No furniture, no lamps, no electronics, no dishes, no knick-knacks—*nada*! Frances had agreed to take the picture albums, knowing that there would be no one to pass them on to.

When Frances finally returned home, she felt exhausted. She realized it wasn't so much the grief but her anger that had made her tired. She was mad! Mad at everything! Mad at her sister for dying of Covid, mad at herself for not taking care of her sister, mad at her nephews for looking at their mother's belongings as trash. Mad at the world! Mad at the news! Mad at male leaders and their bullshit. She was tired.

She looked at the pile of mail sitting on her kitchen table and knew there were unpaid bills in there waiting for her attention. She didn't feel like doing anything except sipping her coffee, lighting up her cigarette, and petting her dogs.

She went ahead and set up her laptop on the porch table in order to go through her emails, which she'd been neglecting for weeks now. As frustration mounted with all of the advertisements and spam, she noticed an email from Doyle with a subject line that read: Sundance in South Dakota. The April trip had come and gone while she was tending to her sister's funeral. She opened the email, and the travel timeline was there on her screen. She closed her eyes and said, "Fuck it. Maybe I can be healed from all this anger and grief inside of me. A ceremony like this is so powerful."

Frances knew that she could make prayer requests for herself while attending. Her mind began to gear up, and the logistics of preparing for a road trip started to fall into place. She would have to deal with being in public and the exposure to Covid. She had just gotten vaccinated and hoped this would shield her from that deadly disease. As she read the email, she vacillated between her reasons for going and not going. Then certainty settled in: This trip was what she wanted, what she *needed* for herself.

The rendezvous would begin in Rapid City in six weeks. The group was going the Highway 90 route, but it would be to her advantage to go on Highway 80. This meant Frances would be driving alone across several states. She figured she could motel it and camp along the way. She reread the timeline, realizing that there would also be pre-ceremony preparations to consider. Questions developed about the details. She realized she needed to call Doyle because he was the person coordinating it. She was totally dependent on his guidance.

"Hi, Doyle," she said when he answered. "Frances here."

"Yup," he said. "What's up? Haven't heard from you for a while."

Noting a tone of indifference in his voice that was new since she'd spoken to him last, she continued to speak. "My sister passed away recently," Frances explained. "I drove down to L.A. to be with my family."

"Oh, that's where you've been? Why didn't you call and let me know? I left a couple of messages, and you didn't return my texts."

"I was so occupied" was all she could offer; she knew it would be too hard for her to explain the silence of her grief. "I apologize."

"Are you still planning on going with us to Sundance? You missed the April trip to South Dakota, so I didn't know if you were still interested."

She could hear in his voice that he was disappointed in her. "Yes, I want to make it," she said. "That's why I'm calling."

"Okay. Well, did you get our emails? There are several regarding the rules and protocols. If you have never been there, you need to know all about the rez. It's a rough place, and you cannot go in without an escort. I know you said earlier you would meet us there. But I'm telling you, it's no place to get lost. We are having a Zoom meeting next week. It's important that you attend. Terri is going to lead it."

"Yes," Frances replied quietly, wondering if she had the energy to do this. "I read the timeline but didn't see any address or contact info in South Dakota."

"Terri is going to cover all that. However, this meeting is about the protocols and understanding why moontime is forbidden. You must know about this? When a woman is on her period. It's absolutely forbidden for ladies in their moontime to attend the ceremony. Some of the women don't know about this. This is really, really important that all the women attending understand this. She is also going to go over what to wear and what not to wear. Do you have a prayer shawl? If not, you better start working on it. How about moccasins? When you are down in the arbor, you need a pair."

"Yeah, I'll get working on what I need, and, yes, I'll be at the meeting." Frances knew that Doyle could talk a lot about everything and anything. But he knew things as a medicine man, and she respected him for that. She just wondered, did he respect her?

"That's great!" Doyle responded. He sounded excited now. "It will be good to have you there. Didn't you say that you were a medicine woman?"

"I don't know if I said that. It's something I don't talk about." Frances realized he had recognized her experience. Maybe he respected her after all?

"Well, they will know if you are," he continued. "I suggest you keep it low-key. The reason you are there is to work at setting up the camp and taking it down. This is not the place to show off your thing, you know what I mean? When I'm in charge, I run a tip-top camp. No one rests. We work. We put up several shade shelters, one for our kitchen—we will be cooking too. We will be putting up some tipis this time for the elders. Are you okay with working?"

"I understand. I'm available to work." Frances replied as her thoughts swirled around about Doyle being a sergeant in the past and this is how they must talk. He had built up a community, and he seemed to get things done. She admired him for that, and she was enjoying feeling that she belonged to a cause or purpose, even if it meant he discounted her as a medicine keeper. All the years of being a *curandera* carried southern traditions. She was entering the northern traditions now. They were new to her, and she had much to learn. She was a newbie to his group and wanted to be humble as she entered the hoop of the Lakota world.

"Remember," Doyle was saying, "like I said before—we are there for one purpose, and that is to support the dancers of this ceremony. We support them with prayer down in the arbor, setting up their camp, making sure they have firewood for their sweats. It's all about them during the ceremony. We don't fraternize with others or make friends. They know you come from the outside and will ask you for things. I've been doing this for a long time. I know what I'm doing."

"Yeah, it's my first time there." Frances agreed with him because he was so confident. She had always thought of herself as street tough and keeping her bitch on, yet when she heard Doyle's voice, she felt unsure of herself. She considered that Doyle may be a good, strong teacher and leader for her—that he could help her rebuild the strength she needed to get her through the next chapter of her life. That perhaps he could use some of her humility, and they could balance each other, meet in the middle by learning from one another.

"I know," said Doyle. "That's why I'm telling you this."

"It's very strict, isn't it?" she asked.

"Yeah. I don't know how many other ceremonies you've been involved in. But, yes, this one holds a lot of power. When you go with me, it's my reputation on the line. That's why I'm so picky with my people because you represent me. Ha! I want everything just right, you know."

"Okay, I got it," said Frances, keeping her responses minimal to avoid setting him off on another tangent. She could see how inflated his ego was, but she didn't want to deal with it, so she shook her head and allowed his comments to roll off her back. "I will see you at the meeting."

"Yeah, good night."

Frances settled into her evening with her dogs nestled around her hips. She petted them and apologized that she would need to leave them with her neighbor once again. Just like cameras were not allowed at the ceremony, she knew that pets weren't either. This was not her first Sundance, but it was her first on Oglala land—her first with the Lakota, keepers of this prayer and wisdom.

Frances pondered for a moment a few things about her conversation with Doyle. There was the fact that he had not offered her his condolences when her sister had been such a big part of her life. There were his assumptions that she needed strict oversight, when she knew she was independent and tough enough to handle a place like Pine Ridge. She felt that perhaps Doyle just wasn't interested enough to know her. His assumptions about her worried her for a bit, but then she discarded these thoughts because she was tired. She decided she would make the most of the ceremony experience, independent of whatever weird dynamic was unfolding with Doyle.

# GUARDIAN OF THE SPRINGS

Frances had dreamed of finding a place someday that would help her unravel and unleash, a place that would spark and nurture the seeds of her tomorrows. This idea had always seemed far-fetched because through all of her travels, no matter how remote, she had always managed to stay composed and grounded. Visiting a new place for the first time was always exciting for her because it held the potential to deliver her to a higher level of consciousness, but she hesitated to place that lofty expectation on this trip. This time, her mission was to work hard to serve the people of the Sundance ceremony. Frances shifted her gears heading east, this time driving to the heart center of Turtle Island. This invitation felt right.

Solo, she drove opposite from the Sun's daily journey until she couldn't. She found herself on the outskirts of Salt Lake City, where the vapor of Mormonism was just a little too thick for her taste. Frances had had some schooling here in her youth, and she remembered the lessons she'd learned here. She had attended her freshman year of college at Brigham Young and had found it way too square and conformist for the expansion she desired from her college studies. Most of the students and professors she met there were clearly uncomfortable with her voice, her queries, and her wardrobe. They didn't know what to make of her headbands, her moccasins, or her striped bell-bottoms. She quickly found herself ostracized and decided that although she was on a full scholarship, it just wasn't worth it to her. She would rather go into debt and study with people who challenged the status quo. But that was Frances, always taking the rough road.

She just wasn't her best in pretentious places, so she decided to push herself and make it up the mountain to Park City, where the air was fresh, and spend the night. The next morning, she quickly gathered her stuff in the motel and then searched Yelp for a breakfast drive-thru where she could get some strong coffee and make her way eastward. The Sun had not made its appearance yet, and dew preoccupied the moment. Colors arrived in the sky as she gave her order to the speaker outside the fast-food joint. "A large coffee with four half-and-half and four sugars and a plain breakfast sandwich—you know, bacon, egg, cheese."

"Do you want to make that a meal? Potatoes come with it," the voice through the intercom said.

"Sure, make it a meal," said Frances. The colors intensified as she pulled up and waited for her first meal of the day. She couldn't be bothered with her GPS and kept her eyes fixed ahead on the sky, watching the rapid change taking place as the Sun was beginning to rise. In this moment, she felt the power and spirit of her beloved Changing Woman emerging as a child in the east. This was the direction Frances's journey was going. Changing Woman would pass her on her westward journey; nonetheless, Frances grinned as she thought about Changing Woman's blessings of growth, letting go, and trusting in herself. Frances loved to start her day with gratitude. She received her breakfast through the window and followed the light of the Sun.

Another driving day lay before her; she hoped to make it to somewhere in Wyoming. All this uncharted adventure made her excited as she played her sixties music on the truck radio. She hadn't told anyone except her neighbor where she was going. She would have told her sister, but Lina was gone, and this made her sad. Her other friends would have told her she was crazy for going alone to South Dakota, but she knew she had to go. There was something there for her, *something*.

Later that day, she pulled into Casper, exhausted. Another motel, another shower, another bed to rest on. She figured she was close enough to make it to Hot Springs, South Dakota, the next day and soak up some healing waters before meeting the group in Rapid City. She had an affinity for hot springs in general, and this place had caught her eye as she'd been mapping out her journey.

Another early morning on the road with a hot coffee banging around on her truck's dashboard led her eastward again. She found a campground close to Moccasin Hot Springs and checked in. The lady at the front desk told her to drive around the lake, but in Frances's eyes, it was a pond at best.

It was still early in the day, and she wasted no time finding the place they call Moccasin Hot Springs. It was a private spa and much fancier than she'd expected. She was given a white cotton robe and towel. A stone pathway lined with gold and violet flowers escorted her to the showers and dressing rooms. Inside, she studied the decorative map of Paha Sapa, the sacred mountains of Lakota Nation (known as the Black Hills to everyone else). From an aerial view, it looked like a great big thumping heart. Turns out it happened to be the approximate geographic center of the United States when you factored in Alaska and Hawaii. She could feel in her bones something different here. Something quite different.

Frances had traveled all over the world and could feel the land wherever she went. This was her first time in South Dakota. She had a feeling here in Paha Sapa that she had been lost and now she was found. The lush green grasses of late spring and early summer, the pine forest, the swollen creeks, the flocks of birds, the bison grazing made a feast for her eyes—but it was her heart that felt big and healthy there. There was a deep down Earth sacredness here, and she surrendered to it, beginning her urge to open up to what lay ahead for her.

Set inside the stone masonry of the nineteenth-century building ruins were several pools. With the ceilings gone, the springs were open to the gentle sunlight of nearby trees. Old rafters were exposed, with verdant vines wrapping themselves around and cascading down to the surface of the water.

The minute she entered the pool, the waters began speaking to her. "Welcome," they whispered.

"Thank you," she replied as she held her breath and submerged her head beneath the heated surface.

She continued to give thanks as she bubbled up and caught her breath. "I am here with you, sacred waters. I am here to pray in the most profound way. I will give my best to honor you today. Take this song as my offering." Frances began softly singing her water song.

A lady nearby heard her and watched Frances complete her offering. The thick, chunky woman with a bleached hairdo then approached Frances and said, "I noticed you singing. Where are you from?"

"I'm from here," Frances answered without giving it any thought.

The woman seemed confused. "Are you American?" she asked.

"Yes, very American," Frances answered.

"Oh, I didn't realize that."

"Why? Don't I look American to you?"

"Well, the song you were singing sounded like a foreign language."

"Oh, it's a Native American song we sing to the waters for blessing."

"You are Native American?"

"Yes, Native to North America. I'm not actually from *here*," Frances clarified. "I'm from California, but I consider myself home here in the United States."

"Oh, I see," the woman said. "Well, I'm from Texas, visiting my sister. She and her husband decided to move here for their retirement. I really like it here."

"That's nice." Frances refrained from giving her opinion about her Texas experience. "Have a stellar day," she said, and began to float away. She wanted to be alone and get away from the banal exchange with this woman.

The woman seemed confused yet assented to Frances's departure. Frances spotted a quiet corner and continued her prayers to the sacred waters. She grounded into the sources of the heated waters, deep down into the crust of the planet. Here she felt Mother Earth at her best, her warm belly hot with desire, bubbling up to the surface—giving her love, and Frances was well enough to receive it. Frances instinctively knew that all hot springs brought healing not only to the physical body but to the spiritual body too. After her prayers were finished, she closed her eyes and continued to feel the depth of Mother Earth. She silently spoke to the Mother, asking her for her blessings to guide her through this journey and her desire to be healed from her grief and anger. A surge of bubbles emerged in the water around her, as if to acknowledge her sincerity.

Frances was left alone for the rest of the day. Her energy seemed to repel noisy tourists as she walked around the small town and found a trail into the wilderness. The forest comforted her, allowing her to feel a connection to her deepest self. The waters had relaxed her and cleansed away her subtle worries, the part of her that resisted the unknown.

In the evening, Frances returned to her camp and began to set up her bed inside her tent. She instinctively knew how to make it soft and cozy with a high-tech, self-inflating air mattress and a memory foam layer, a soft cotton blanket under her, and her favorite faux fur blanket over her. She was tired, and she couldn't wait to go horizontal. But the moment her head rested on her pillow, she began to cry.

Confused, she asked herself, *Why? Why am I crying?*

The tears grew bigger until her face felt like a waterfall. "Aggggh! What is happening?" She grabbed for something to clean her face with.

The tears continued; now the sobbing was bubbling up from her gut. She could not stop this feeling of sadness overpowering her. *Why?* Was it the waters she had visited today? The tears felt hot like the water spirits, and her gut felt like throwing up. *Maybe I shouldn't go to Rapid City tomorrow. Maybe this is not for me. What am I doing here? What is my purpose here? I asked for healing. What else is it that needs to be released?* These were the thoughts that bounced in her head and her heart.

She cried some more and eventually fell asleep.

# REVERED MOTHER'S BREATH

Frances woke up that next morning refreshed and relaxed. Figuring it was about six, she unzipped her tent and took a peek outside. The Sun was strong, yet the pond revealed a thin layer of fog on its surface. It seemed to be evaporating right before her eyes. The songs of the feathered ones were above, hidden in the tree branches. She felt so different from the night before; she took a moment to smile and rub her eyes. All she had was a moment, for she knew she had a long day ahead.

Doyle had texted her several times over the last few days, but she had not bothered to send replies. She figured she would arrive at the designated time. She would keep her word, and that would be enough.

Since this was the day she would meet up with the group in Rapid City, she figured it was time for her to respond—after taking care of herself with a morning prayer; a good, strong cup of coffee; and a savory breakfast. It took some time to gather her things and deconstruct her tent, but the timing looked good to her as she departed. She had all day to visit the National Park between her and Rapid City. She had come across the origin story of the Lakota with regard to the Wind Cave, and she wanted to leave an offering of tobacco before entering the rez.

While she was finishing up her breakfast at a quaint cafe she found in town, she decided to connect with Doyle. It was nice and quiet, the perfect time to ruffle his feathers. The young waitress brought her bill and refilled her coffee cup. She pulled out her phone from her backpack and checked for messages. Seeing a string of unread texts from Doyle, she snickered devilishly. She knew he would be upset with her. She began typing.

> Frances: Morning Doyle ✺ how is everything? What is your ETA for this evening in Rapid City?

> Doyle: Where have you been?

Before Frances could respond, her phone rang and she picked up. "Hi, Frances here."

She heard heightened urgency in Doyle's voice. "How come you don't answer my texts? I have no idea what you are doing. I'm trying to keep all this shit together."

"You said we were meeting tonight in Rapid City," she responded. "That's why I'm contacting you. I'm here in Hot Springs, a few hours away."

He sounded annoyed. "Oh, great. *Now* you let me know. What are you planning to do? I still have to go to Walmart and Menards and pick up some supplies. We got about twelve hours ahead of us. We've been driving since six this morning. I wanted to get on the road earlier, but herding everyone this morning was like chasing chickens, I tell you."

"You sound stressed," Frances said with a smirk.

"Well, not all of us have the luxury of enjoying Hot Springs. Was it nice?"

Frances took another sip of her coffee and pulled the phone away, wondering about his sarcasm as she formulated her reply. "Yes, actually. Very nice. So, what is your ETA? I'll meet you at Walmart tonight."

"I hope you are not planning on going inside the rez before we do," said Doyle. "Like I said, it's no place to get lost."

"I said I'll meet you tonight," Frances repeated.

"Okay, let's meet at eight at the parking lot of Walmart, and we will all go together from there." He just couldn't seem to leave it alone. "And be there! And keep your phone close by."

Grimacing at the phone, Frances replied, "Yeah, see you then."

It was clear that Doyle was mad at her. She had not felt this from him before, perhaps disappointment, but not anger. She felt concerned because she didn't want to start off the event this way. She figured he was triggered by her independence and nonchalant attitude as well as the stress from the long drive. She hoped that once they made it safe and sound, everything would be better.

Sitting in her truck, she pulled out her atlas and found the location of the Wind Cave. Ten miles up the road, and that day's journey would begin. On the way, she noticed a herd of wild buffalo in the rolling hills at the park's entrance. She had known this trip would reveal these magnificent primordial beasts that had ruled the land for millennia and coexisted with the native peoples of this continent. They were beings of legend. They were here after all the attempts to eradicate them. Like her, they belonged to the land they'd evolved from. She wondered what a stampede sounded like in the distance and the message it sent to the subsurface of the Earth. What did it send out to the atmosphere? She listened for an echo.

Frances began to cry again and felt a bit fuzzy, but she started her drive anyway. When she approached the signs pointing her to the Wind Cave parking lots, Frances was surprised to see crowds of people walking around the entrance of the park's welcome center. *What a bummer*, she thought. Would she have to stand in these long lines? After entering the building, she approached a young female ranger with long, thick hair and a smile that seemed friendly.

"Hi," Frances began. "I was hoping to see the Wind Cave today."

"Yes, it's pretty popular today," said the ranger. "It's that time of year, you know."

"Do I need a ticket?" asked Frances.

The ranger pulled out a map from a stand nearby and opened it. "Those lines outside the door are for the tours," she told Frances. "If you'd like, you can go on your own. It's easy to find—right outside those two doors. About a quarter mile, stay on the path, you can't miss it. If you get up close, you can feel the cool winds coming from inside the earth. It's really nice on a hot day like today."

"That's easy," said Frances, reassured. "Thanks for your help."

She took the map and headed toward the doors, wondering if the ranger had actually winked at her or if it had been her imagination. Following the path, Frances found the entrance to the cave. It was much smaller than she'd expected—maybe two or three feet in diameter? And where was everybody? Frances realized she was alone there with the cave. She walked down several cement steps and understood the gift she'd been given of time and space to leave her offering of tobacco.

She approached the cave with her way of reverence before

stepping in to feel the wind. It was cold, crisp, and powerful as it touched her skin. She stood still and closed her eyes as the current of this underground air encircled her, and she opened herself to what felt like a blessing from the Earth itself.

When she opened her eyes, a smile emerged because she was still alone with the Wind Cave. She grabbed a handful of tobacco from the fringed leather pouch she wore across her shoulder. She blew her love and gratitude into the tobacco and placed it on a rock beneath the cave's entrance. Her hat blew off, and she giggled as she went to retrieve it across the paved pathway—still alone.

She could have stayed in that spot all day for the happiness it brought her. But then Frances began to hear the voices of the tour group and decided it was time for her to make her way north through Paha Sapa.

She followed the signs to Rapid City, weaving her way through all the summer traffic. The small towns seemed to her like tourist traps, with large billboards marking the way toward the interstate. When she passed the entrance to Mount Rushmore, a reaction arose in her like most people react when they see beautiful art or architecture defaced. This was the worst example of imposing the message of manifest destiny on a natural precipice she could think of, transforming an awe-inspiring rock cliff into a carnival attraction. God forbid someone would think of carving up the beauty of her beloved Half Dome in California. Her happiness began to dissolve the more she had to wait in traffic.

Frances eventually made it out of that mess and came into the foothills of the mountains. She wished she would have been able to drive through more forest like the curved and narrow roads of her Sierras. She realized that based on the traffic patterns and hordes of tourists she had just passed, evidently, some people in her country actually liked the plastic artificiality of amusement parks.

Her hunger began to overrule her thoughts, and she figured it would be a good time to get something to eat. She had a couple of hours to kill before meeting up with Doyle.

Frances arrived in the Walmart parking lot thirty minutes before the appointed meeting time. She drove around, and then, surmising that the group had not arrived yet, she parked and texted Doyle.

Frances: "I'm here at Walmart."

Doyle: "Good, stay there. We are about half an hour away."

Frances replied with a thumbs-up emoji. Everything seemed copacetic. There was a beautiful sunset emerging, so she stepped outside her vehicle and lit up a cigarette while she waited. Eventually, the caravan of a truck and a large passenger van pulled up next to her and parked. This was the first time she would meet the group in person instead of at Zoom meetings.

Everyone seemed exhausted as they stepped out onto the parking lot. Doyle approached her first and said, "Wow, what a drive! Ha! You are here!"

"I said I would be," she answered.

"Yeah, but you are always off on another planet! Ha! It's good to see you." Even though he seemed exhausted, he just had to dig into her. It didn't matter to her, though, as she was relaxed and fed. It had turned out to be a lovely day.

He smiled and turned around to gather the rest of the group. "Gather around and let's talk about what we need to pick up here. Terri, do you have that list?"

Frances had seen Terri before on Zoom, but she seemed older

in person. Perhaps it was because she was tired. She walked over with her backpack and said, "Yes, I've got it. I'll meet you inside. I have to use the restroom. Excuse me." She nodded toward Frances before walking toward the store.

The other ladies retrieved their fanny packs from the van, some approaching Frances to introduce themselves or say they recognized her from online meetings. One of them suggested that they should use the restroom, too, since they still had a long way to go. Frances agreed and walked over to lock her truck. She turned and counted five women who all seemed to be in their thirties or forties—much younger than her and very pale in skin tone. She wasn't surprised by this, as that was her impression of people who live in the Pacific Northwest. She would be the only Native woman in the group. She felt odd at first because of her elder status and ethnicity. Strange that these white girls were more seasoned in Native American traditions than she was. Still, she hoped to bond with them camping and working hard in the next week or so—to develop another Women's Circle like she enjoyed doing. Sisterhood was important to her, no matter what color of skin someone wore.

After the group completed their errands, they drove off toward the Badlands and Pine Ridge, with Frances joining the caravan. The darkness of night had consumed the orange and purple sunset. What struck her while driving was the intensity of the Milky Way and the stars flooding the dark night with their brilliance. It was too dark to see the bizarre landscape of the Badlands, but she felt something spooky here.

It was close to midnight when they arrived at their destination. Doyle pulled off the paved road onto a steep gravel road. They passed a few hills before coming to the end of the road. There were a few houses with porch lights lit up. Doyle parked and got out of his truck to instruct the other drivers about where to park.

Everyone emerged from the vehicles and made signs of relief, stretching and yawning at the same time. Doyle pointed out a trailer home next to where they had parked and announced, "This is where we camp, where we use the bathroom, showers, kitchen. Got it?" then kept speaking without waiting to receive the group's assent. "The chief lives across the road there. Set up your tents along the side here, and I'll see you in the morning. It's been a long day, and everyone did good. We made it safe and sound."

The next morning, she crawled out the back of her truck to see, for the first time, the interior of this rez they called Pine Ridge. There were rolling hills and a creek near the trailer home and, beyond, a grove of tall trees surrounded by tall grasses. She spotted two other houses beyond the grove of trees, but nothing else but wilderness before her. The Sun had already risen above the horizon, and Frances realized she was still tired from last night's activities.

What broke her sleep—besides the bright sunlight coming through her truck's back window—was Doyle's loud voice. She heard a commotion of some sort with some of the ladies in the group. She rustled herself up and walked toward the trailer home where Doyle had set up his belongings. As she walked toward the door, she heard something about coffee not being made and other things about breakfast not being made. *It can't be nine yet—maybe eight?* she thought to herself. She offered to make coffee and get breakfast ready as the others were walking away toward their tents. "I can help with that," she said. "No need to get upset."

They just looked at her with perplexed expressions. One of the women turned toward her and said, "We are having a meeting in fifteen minutes inside the house."

# SMELLS WITH ITS TONGUE

There was an air of disappointment coming from Doyle as Frances made her way into the main living space of the trailer home. It was strange that this energy hung low around her feet. Everyone was quiet as Doyle began talking about how things were not getting done in a timely manner—that they were there to work, and if everyone was getting up late, how was that going to happen? One lady interjected and said it wouldn't happen again.

Doyle began to read off a list of things that needed to happen that day. The group would need to prepare tent poles for the tipis so the elders could have their space. This was a priority. Sun shelters also needed to be put up. Volunteers had to make dinner for the group. He finished by saying that he needed to go back into town for some hardware and that he expected it to all be done by the time he got back. He did mention again not to socialize with the locals, reminding the group about this being like a Third World nation and all they had covered in the "Rez 101" prep talks at their Zoom meetings. Everyone seemed so unhappy as Frances studied their faces. She thought to herself, *what a terrible way to start our service to the ceremony.* He then reminded the ladies in the group not to wear any jewelry, nail polish, make-up, bright colors, perfumes—and especially no essential oils because these scents gave him a headache. Then he walked toward his truck and drove off.

Frances approached the group, but from the way the other women avoided eye contact, it was apparent to her that she was barely accepted. Perhaps it was because she was from a different area; maybe it was something Doyle had said about her. She wasn't able to figure it out just yet, but they were probably the most unfriendly people she had ever met.

She approached them anyway and said, "Look, I just want to be useful."

Megan, one of the gals, replied, "Yeah, it's a little more complicated than you know. We will start this up soon." This comment left Frances wondering what she was missing in their relationship with Doyle—a history among them that excluded her.

Frances could tell that the morale of the group was pretty low. She wondered why they were even there. What was their commitment to this Native American ceremony? Was it a personal desire to right the wrong of an American genocide that had rid the Native people from their own land? Or perhaps they desired to have a Native American man (whom she saw from time to time because these men carried a great deal of spiritual mystery)?

Where was the joy of coming together? One of her teachers, an elder auntie, had told her that ceremonies should begin with laughter because it raises the vibration to enter the portal of the spirit world. A song, a grateful prayer of being alive, flowers, beautiful bright clothing, and joy were the offerings to this mythic realm. This situation, however, had shades of her Catholic upbringing, where the ceremonies were imbued with confessions of sin and slaps on the face by the bishop. So much colonial bullshit, and here she was again.

She knew that two of the older gals had been to other Sundance ceremonies in the past. From the Zoom meetings, Frances had gathered that non-Native people were not allowed to dance at this particular ceremony. When Doyle had introduced her at the Zoom meeting, he'd mentioned that Frances should be taught Lakota songs by Megan and Terri because they had been allowed to be Sundancers in other ceremonies. Frances would probably become the only Sundancer in this group besides Doyle. Frances disagreed with him to be a dancer because she knew it was an arduous sacrifice of oneself to be a Sundancer. Physically, mentally, and spiritually, she would have to train for it like a warrior—not a battle warrior but a prayer warrior. At her age, she would have preferred the softer training of women's medicine. This was the initial reason she had signed up to join this group—to learn plant medicines and earth songs, to help nurture future generations. She was no spring chicken, and she knew her limitations.

Looking back, Frances could see that there had been times during the Zoom meetings when Doyle had shown her preferential treatment. She considered that perhaps the other women could be jealous of her. She wasn't involved with him in an intimate way, but perhaps they were, or wanted to be. She could see that it was somehow complicated.

Lost in these reflections, Frances noticed that one of the women was approaching to speak with her. This younger woman with large hazel eyes and mid-length blond hair under the triangle of a blue bandana said to her, "Turn around. See that flatbed trailer over there? See that stack of long tree trunks? He wants us to take the bark off. They are still green, so it's going to be messy. I suggest we get started soon."

Instinctively, Frances tilted her shoulders and head and gave the blondie snake eyes. Anyone could read the look on Frances's face, that look like *don't fuck with me*. Frances dismissed her by saying, "Wait—has anyone had breakfast?" They all looked at her, then walked out of the room one by one without responding. Frances had their number and decided she was going to have to take care of herself. She was grateful for her independence.

Frances followed them outside and decided to have her breakfast anyway. She knew her body well and knew that she needed to eat something before she tackled the day's agenda. Her truck had everything she needed to be self-reliant. She started on an apple while she put together a tuna sandwich from her ice chest. Coffee was necessary; she went ahead and pulled out her portable stove and coffee kit.

From the back of her truck, Frances could see the group walking toward the lower meadow to the flatbed trailer. She noticed the blue bandana gal carrying scraping tools, and the others carrying axes and tool bags. She muttered to herself, "*Qué pendejas*, it's going to be a long day, and they are working without fuel. Aye, youngsters."

The aroma of her coffee brewing hit its apex, and a younger Lakota man smoking his cigarette near the house trailer said to her, "Sure does smell nice. If you have a little extra, I'll take some of that."

Frances turned around to face him. "Oh, morning!" she said. "Sure. Got a cup?"

"Really, I was just kidding," he chuckled.

"I'm not," she said. "Get it while it's fresh."

The man went inside the house trailer and came back out with a coffee cup. "How's that?"

As she began to pour the brew in his cup, she said, "Hi, my name is Frances."

"Hi," he responded. "My name is Gerald. Hey, thanks."

"Yeah, absolutely. Do you live close by?" Frances asked because she had not seen him around since she'd arrived. She was aware of the chief's house up the road and had seen curious children on the road earlier.

Gerald turned around and pointed to the trailer home.

"You live there?" she asked, surprised.

"Yup." He nodded.

"Wow! We have been in your space this whole time, and I just meet you by accident out here," Frances said with genuine embarrassment.

"Don't worry about it," Gerald said as he sipped his coffee.

"Cookies? Sandwich? Apple?" she offered. "Wow, you're the first person I've met here! Oglala?"

He cracked up, then just smiled at her and reached out for a handful of Oreos instead of answering. He knew she had figured it out. She sipped her coffee and smiled back. They sat in silence for a bit, feeling each other out in an indigenous way. Gerald then asked, "What brand are you?"

Recognizing the humorous way Natives would refer to one another, Frances answered, "I'm a California Native, Tongva or Chumash. Chicana, you know."

"Whoa, that's a mouthful!" said Gerald. "Never heard of that! They have Natives out there in California? I thought there were only surfers and techies out there."

"No, we got Cholos and Lowriders out there too. Ha."

"Ah man, you one of those? I've seen them on the internet. Interesting cats."

"Yup, I'm from the cement rez. But now I'm in your rez."

"You got that right."

There was an air of respect that Frances had learned from growing up Chicana—respect for anyone whose house you entered and respect for yourself. It didn't matter to her what Doyle said about not speaking to the locals. He didn't know her.

She gathered her portable kitchen and straightened the back of her truck before driving it down to the lower meadow and joining the group. No one seemed to notice her as she watched what they were doing. She spotted the scrapers in the back of the flatbed trailer and went to work without exchanging a word with them.

Later that day, Frances found herself exhausted by the heat of the midday prairie sun and her own tired muscles. She had been scraping bark off the tipi poles for a few hours now. She looked up and could feel the others' exhaustion. She needed a break and something to drink. Frances's way was always to share the food she had with anyone in her proximity. There was always enough, and it seemed to her like this was just general good manners. It was also a custom she had come across while visiting Polynesian cultures. Strangers would invite her into their homes to eat; over her objections, they would insist, and she would end up making friends for life.

She went to the back of her truck and pulled out her cooler. In a loud voice, she said, "Hey, everybody! I have plenty of cold drinks here and some snacks too. Come get it while it's ice-cold."

A woman about Frances's age, with a long purple skirt, short grey hair, and wrinkles around her eyes, exclaimed, "Yeah, I need a break!

This sun is intense." She dropped her tool on the ground, wiped her brow, and began walking toward the back of Frances's truck.

The others were hesitant but began to put their tools down and trek in the direction of Frances's generosity. Some of them placed the cold cans right on their foreheads or the backs of their sweaty necks before opening the drinks. Each expressed thanks and agreed that it was necessary to take a break. The sun's heat was becoming unbearable.

There were two young men in the group; one was Doyle's nephew she had met the night before, and the other was a local. The younger one suggested that perhaps they should work on the two shade structures, and then they would have shade to work under. Some of the group agreed, but some didn't. It turned out that these shade structures were carports, and they would need everyone's help to secure them to the ground. They needed everyone to participate if this task was going to move forward.

Frances spotted Doyle's truck coming up the road. He drove around the work area and idled his truck, shouting out the window, "Is that it? That's all the poles that are done? You've got to be kidding me!" Then he drove off.

Frances watched him as he drove toward the far end of the meadow near the arbor. She had just busted her ass off scraping bark off lodge poles in the heat of the day and felt like smacking that *puto*. She could tell she was very different from the other women in the group because Doyle's behavior did not seem to bother them. She wondered if perhaps she was involved in some sort of cult. She never saw women so damn docile.

From a distance, Frances could see a tall, thin man climbing into the passenger seat of Doyle's truck. The truck turned around and started driving back toward the crew. Doyle parked and the two men hopped out. "Hey, everyone," said Doyle. "Take a break and come meet the chief."

The chief was much younger than Frances had expected. He was tall, with a thin man's gait, and he wore two long braids under a baseball hat. He lifted his arm and rounded his hand to gesture for everyone to come over. "Put your things down for a minute," said Doyle. "This won't take long."

As soon as everyone was present, the chief introduced himself. He welcomed everyone and thanked them for their help. He went over some house rules and Sundance ceremony protocols. He then expressed how much respect he had for his wife—how she was in charge of the kitchen and of feeding the people who came to pray, how she made three meals a day. He said he would appreciate it if each and every one of the crew helped out and made it easy for her. He said she also would like to come down to the arbor and be present. "Welcome, again," he said in conclusion. "Remember, no what?"

"No cameras!" some answered.

"No moontime gals," others added.

"Right on," he replied, and began to walk toward the truck, then turned around. "Oh yeah, I almost forgot! We have an *inipi* ceremony tomorrow night. In case you are not familiar with this, it's our sweat lodge for purification, and everyone must attend. There will be one for the ladies and one for the men. After that, we are having a potluck at my house. I hope to see everyone gathered."

Frances took notice of the chief's leadership and felt comfortable with it. He wasn't asking for too much, yet he inspired everyone to play their part and enjoy one another as family and revere this profound ceremony for the next week. He seemed like a balanced human. She was impressed by the respect he gave to his wife; it was a marked contrast from Doyle's lack of respect toward the women in the group. With Doyle, it seemed as if any effort from his posse was never enough and certainly not appreciated. Frances just wanted to feel peace here but couldn't because her values and integrity were not being respected.

There was a definite shift with the chief's presence that day, a firm leadership that was both humorous and serious at the same time. He had the energy of a good father who took care of his people. She could tell he brought a sort of relief to the group with his inclusiveness and gratitude for their help. Everyone around her seemed at ease now.

She scanned the horizon of the plains before her and saw flatlands and thunderheads in the distance, much different from the mountain horizon she was accustomed to. It was happening. This feeling was the reason Frances had desired to come to Pine Ridge for this ceremony.

There was activity all around her. Lakota families had set up their tents with shade structures in proximity to the center of the ceremonial grounds. Her camp seemed to be the farthest away from the families. She had an idea why: because Doyle did not want his group to be close to them. She listened to the laughter of beautiful children running around poking prairie dog holes with any sticks they could find. Down by the arbor, Lakota women were on ladders placing limbs of pine branches above the rafters for shade. A group of teenage boys was erecting tipi poles and placing canvas covers over them with skill. Men were chopping up firewood. Trucks had arrived and were dropping off large plastic bins in front of the outdoor kitchen area. It was surreal to her, like a living painting.

She was beginning to feel like her Native American heart somehow belonged here.

Frances was returning to her truck to have a smoke and something to snack on when she noticed the woman with the purple skirt had squatted between some parked cars and was crying. Frances instinctively approached her and asked, "Is there anything I can help with?"

The woman looked up and shook her head no.

"How about something cold to drink?" With this kindness from Frances, the woman's emotions seemed to shift, and they both began to giggle. Using her skirt to wipe her tears away, the woman agreed and got up to follow Frances toward the truck.

"You are very kind," she told Frances as she picked out a grape soda from the ice chest. "I like you."

"You seem kind yourself," Frances responded; she had noticed earlier that this woman also smiled, smoked cigarettes, and kept her distance from the others. "Are you from Washington too?"

"No, I'm from around here," she answered. "I'm from Nebraska, just down the road. By the way, I'm Judith."

"I'm Frances. I don't think I've ever met someone from Nebraska."

"Yup, born and raised, as Nebraska as you get! I'm so sorry to pull you into my drama," Judith continued, "but sometimes he makes me so mad! Telling me things that I just don't agree with."

"Who?" asked Frances. "Who's telling you what?"

"You know, Doyle told me to turn off my phone for the rest of the week, that I didn't need to be talking to anybody. He caught me talking to my husband when the chief was here. I told him I needed to talk to Gary before he took off on his trip with my son."

"I understand no cameras, but no phones?" Frances questioned.

"Yeah, he just doesn't understand that I'm very close to my family. I'm hardly ever away from them."

"I understand," said Frances, puffing on her cigarette while both of them looked ahead in silence.

Frances knew that something was going to have to change. If she couldn't go along with the group's ways of low self-esteem, either she would have to take on a women's leadership role to balance it out or she'd need to leave the group altogether. Wasn't that what her dreams, her visions, her spiritual guides had been telling her? She looked up to the sky and saw mammatus clouds colored in soft lavender. It was a very feminine phenomenon she had never seen or felt. She trusted that Changing Woman was there with her, allowing her to witness that change, whatever it was.

The hard work of the day seemed to bring everyone together for the evening. Doyle had made a pot of spaghetti with garlic bread and a salad. Everyone agreed it was delicious. It was the first time they all had seemed at ease.

After dinner, fighting their exhaustion, they managed to take their turns for showers and crawl into their tents. While Frances was waiting, she smoked her cigarette and gazed at the brilliance of the stars. The prairie was new to her, yet it felt so familiar. She could hear the coyotes—or perhaps they were wolves?—in the distance. This was the land of Ptesanwin, White Buffalo Calf Woman. Ptesanwin gave her people the *channunpa*, the sacred cere-monial pipe, each part of it symbolizing the elements and natural world. The stem, the bowl, the smoke, and the blend of herbs honored the link between the people and the spirit world. Frances laid tobacco on the ground in immense gratitude for being there.

She asked for Ptesanwin's guidance as she did every day when she prayed for trust.

The next day, everyone gathered for the morning meeting, cups of coffee in hand. Doyle mainly discussed the pressure he was under trying to get this group to do what they were supposed to do. He said they would have to move their tents closer to the shade structures—and who had placed the structures there anyway? The poles were a priority—therefore, get them done. He reminded them that there was a potluck later and said the women had better start cooking up.

Frances observed how everyone sat in silence and no one questioned him. So she did: "So will you be here to help us peel bark today? We could use an extra set of hands if you want things done in time."

Doyle seemed a bit surprised by her question and said, "No, I have to go to the airport and pick up some of our guests." The meeting broke up. Frances didn't want to cause trouble, so she kept to herself, picked up a tool, and began working on another lodgepole.

The morale of the group was mixed, and most just picked their own thing to do for the rest of the day. About midday, Frances had gone into the trailer house to fix her lunch when she heard a knock at the back door.

Frances opened the door and saw a Lakota family standing there: a tall, striking middle-aged woman and man who Frances assumed was her husband, along with a young boy of seven or eight wearing a baseball cap and a blue plaid shirt, holding the hand of a small girl who had crescent eyes just like his. "Hi," the woman said to Frances. "The chief said we could take showers here."

"Sure! Come on in," Frances replied as she swung the door

wide open. "The shower is in that room." As they walked inside, she noticed that the man was tall and dark, with a distinguished jaw and a pronounced, pointed nose; he also had those dark-brown crescent eyes. These were the classic features Frances had seen on coins and historical photos—a reminder that she was on their land, the land of their ancestors. None of them made eye contact with her, but they nodded politely. They all headed down the hallway, and Frances returned to the kitchen area.

She gathered her sandwich ingredients, laying out extra bread. The kitchen was so abundant with groceries that the crew had brought in that it looked like it could feed an army. Some time later, the tall Lakota woman came down the hallway with the two children. They looked nice, shiny and silky. Their hair was still wet. The little boy tugged at the woman's shirt and said, "Grandma, I'm hungry."

The woman turned her head down toward him and hushed him a bit, then said, "When your grandpa finishes, I'll make you your lunch."

Frances said, "I was just making *my* lunch and wondered if you would like some ham and cheese sandwiches. I have plenty." She had placed a box of chip bags with flavors she had never heard of on top of one of the kitchen chairs. She realized this was what the little boy had had in mind when he'd said he was hungry. "Please join me. I make good sandwiches."

The Lakota woman had combed her hair into a slick ponytail, and her features had become much more prominent. Her forehead, her cheeks, and her chin held with pride, her dark eyes locked on Frances's for the first time. They each cracked a small grin, and the woman hesitantly accepted Frances's invitation.

"My name is Frances," she ventured.

"My name is Yvonne," said the woman. "This is Carl, and this one is Sandra."

"I saw you earlier out by the arbor."

"Yes, we have been camping there for a few days," said Yvonne.

"It's been so hot," said Frances. "I'm still adjusting to this heat."

"Are you from Alaska or something? Where it's cold?"

"I come from California near the mountains. It gets hot in the summer, but this is intense!"

"First time here?"

"Yes. Do you like mayonnaise? Mustard? Lettuce? Tomatoes? Pickles? Oh, I have some Swiss or cheddar too, somewhere. Some sprouts too. Gotta eat them or they will go bad."

Yvonne answered, "Just mayonnaise, ham, and yellow cheese. Did you say pickles? I'll take one on the side. One for my husband too. Just plain for the kids. They can share a half sandwich."

Frances placed the finished sandwiches on paper plates and handed them out to Yvonne and her family. The children selected their flavors of chips, also asking their grandmother which one she would like. Frances pointed out the ice cooler and told them to pick out their drinks. The woman's husband walked into the kitchen and saw that everyone was eating. A big grin emerged, and he said, "What's for lunch?"

Yvonne giggled and said, "Tell her what you want in your sandwich. You might like all that stuff! Pickles and sprouts."

Frances realized the grandfather had missed the introductions. "Hi! My name is Frances," she said.

"Hi," he responded. "I'm Kenneth. Yeah, what you got? Put it all in there." They all laughed together.

As Frances sat with the family and ate, two women from the crew walked in and seemed startled. The woman with the bandana was one of them. She gave Frances an uncomfortable look, and Frances liked it. It was as if she was in trouble and had some explaining to do. Frances could feel it in her bones. She figured some attention from the crew was better than no attention at all, since many of them seemed determined to treat her as invisible. Frances didn't care anymore and was out to break Doyle's so-called protocols. She was fraternizing with a Lakota family her own way.

"Would you like a sandwich?" Frances asked the women from Doyle's crew. "All the makings are there."

The bandana woman replied, "You do know that we still have a lot of work to do, right?" Then they pulled some protein bars from a box and cold plastic water bottles from the cooler and headed back out the door.

It was confirmed that Frances was in trouble. She smiled and said to the family, "Yeah, well, I've got to eat. Nothing's going to get done without some sandwiches!"

The sunlight from the window shifted, and the metal jar lids caught her eye. On the table, there was a case of homemade pickled salmon Doyle had brought as gifts for the elders and Sundancers.

Frances was well aware of the taboo Doyle had placed on the crew about interacting with the Lakota families. "You're here to work and not engage with them," he had repeatedly reminded them over the last few days. Frances disliked that word: *them*. Why *them*? What the fuck is *them*? What does that mean, anyway? Why not *us*? Aren't we all the same—humans?

Frances said to herself, *Fuck it. Nobody tells me how to treat other humans. I'm a big girl. I can handle it. Besides, I like getting to know these folks. They're genuine, and we laugh together.*

She walked over to the table and picked up a jar of salmon. "Are you a Sundancer?" she asked Kenneth. "I was told that these jars were reserved for the Sundancers. Would you like one?"

Kenneth's eyes lit up and he said, "Sure! I'll need a fork." He didn't wait for Frances to ask again; as he spoke, he was already removing the lid with his personal knife. Everyone watched him as he ate the entire contents of the jar. When he finished, he said, "Delicious! Can I have another?" and everyone cracked up.

"Sure!" Frances replied as she grabbed another jar and handed it to him. "If I'm going to be in trouble, I might as well be in *big* trouble." She knew this was an opportunity for change; she was taking a leadership role without permission from anybody. Besides, she was supporting the dancers like they were instructed to do—only doing it her own way.

"Yeah, I could see that," said Yvonne. "They make food for the kitchen, but they don't eat with us. I wondered if he thinks we bite or something."

Frances said, "Yeah, well, I'm not like that!"

"Uh, you are a rebel!" They all laughed together, and Yvonne continued: "What are you doing with him?"

"I came to learn women's ways."

"From who?"

"One of the elders?" Frances said tentatively. "I think her name is Ruth Leigh? She hasn't arrived yet."

"Oh, I see. Yes, she is one of our elders. Well, thank you for the lunch. Good to meet you," said Yvonne and gestured to her family to thank the lady who had just fed them.

Frances had stopped working later that afternoon because it was time for her beloved cup of coffee and a cigarette, a cookie or two to make it special. As she aged, afternoons had become her respite to get her through her evenings, especially if it was going to be an active evening. She lay down in the back of her truck for a bit before heading to the trailer house kitchen and began to straighten, clean, and gather ingredients for dinner.

Later that evening, the crew returned to the trailer house. Most of them looked exhausted from spending hours peeling the bark off the green trees and making headway on Doyle's to-do list. They washed up and began chopping vegetables in the kitchen; they still had to make soup for the potluck that night.

Frances and Judith, her Nebraskan friend, were sitting outside the house smoking their cigarettes when Yvonne's grandchildren approached them and said in a relaxed tone, "My grandmother needs your help." So Frances and Judith followed the children to their grandmother down by the creek. There was a large willow hedge between the house and creek that kept the Lakota women hidden.

There, they found Yvonne, her sister Tia, and several children sitting near a campfire, cooking up a stew and what looked like dough balls on a tray.

"Hey, you girls want to know the teachings of Lakota women's wisdom?" Yvonne asked. "You can start here. I'm going to teach you how we make our buffalo stew and fry bread. Okay?"

"Yes, ma'am," replied both Frances and Judith.

Yvonne handed Frances a large spoon tied to a straight branch with its limbs cut off. "Here. Start stirring it, and I will hand over the ingredients. We pick the wild ingredients ourselves."

"This just blows me away!" Frances said as she began to stir.

Food is cultural, and of course women's ways would begin over a stovetop. She was eager to ask about the ingredients and learn something new.

Judith asked if anybody would like some water. Everyone said yes, and Judith had started walking up toward the house when Doyle's discordant voice rang out. "Who in the fuck took those jars of salmon? Who?! And who opened that box of chips? That's for the outdoor kitchen during the week!"

Frances peeked around the hedge, and Doyle spotted her. He began walking toward her, his face red and his gait rushed. With the spoon in hand, she took a few steps toward him. Just as he was about to start yelling at Frances, as he did all the other gals, Yvonne and her sister stood up from behind the hedge, and Yvonne said, "Oh, so nice of you to join us, Doyle! I'm teaching the girls Lakota women's wisdom. Isn't that what they are here for? They are doing such a great job!"

Doyle stopped dead in his tracks, for once at a loss for words. He silently pushed a hand toward the sky, then turned around and walked back toward the house. They laughed at him and continued to learn the way of fry bread.

# SHEDDING ITS SKIN

A few nights later, the mighty and forceful prairie winds flattened Frances's tent while she was trying to sleep. She decided to grab her pillow and sleeping bag, crawl underneath her cot for shelter, and sleep on the ground. She knew instinctively that there was nothing she could do in the middle of the night with wind gusts clocking in at forty-five to fifty miles per hour. Her mind was busy, yet she managed to fall asleep.

It was still dark when she heard the bison walking through the camp. It sounded like there were thousands. She froze in fear. She could feel their massiveness all around her. As she lay there, stiff as a fallen branch, she recalled the tender orange and purple mammatus clouds that had floated above her a couple of days earlier. Remembering the embrace of Changing Woman, she managed to doze off once more.

She woke again to the sound of voices just outside her tent and noticed that the Sun had not yet arrived to light up the morning. A song so beautiful was being sung in the dark. Her soul recognized it, but her ears did not. She listened to the whole song before trying to untangle her way out of her tent. When she did eventually emerge, she saw the silhouettes of her campmates headed toward the arbor.

As Frances inhaled, she began to recall a dream from the night. She had seen a young man standing proud with his sword. He had been headed into conflict. Knowing the hardship of wars, she had asked him if he was scared. He'd said, "Of course I am."

Frances had asked him, "Why, then?"

He'd replied, "Because of the Queen of the Earth. I'm in service to her. Her verdant ways, her water ways, her mountainous ways, her atmospheric ways are in peril."

"How can you stop it?" Frances had asked him. "You are only one."

He'd smiled gently and said, "Yes, and so are *you* only one. Together we are one, as it should be. The Queen is one. The many are one for what is before us."

Frances found herself standing alone in the dim moonlight, facing the golden grasses of the flat terrain before her. She gathered herself, slipped on her maroon ribbon skirt and her prayer shawl. She favored this skirt over the others she had made for herself.

She tried to understand the dream's meaning, yet the task before her was too overwhelming. She wanted to be present in the arbor as the Sundancers began their prayer dance and the Sun took its cue. All the preparations were complete; now the Sundancers would follow the beat of the drums for the next four days—four being sacred like the four seasons, four elements, four cardinal directions, and four phases of one's life: child, adolescent, adult, and elder. The dance was a prayer, and it seemed to Frances that the dancers were like stars in the Universe rotating around the Sun.

Smoke rose from tin pots burning sage at the perimeter of the arbor's circle. She walked over toward one of the pots and gathered the smoke around her body. It was another form of purification for her to begin her day with. Her deep connection to the Earth's power and the eternal force of the Universe had never felt brighter or stronger. When the Sun appeared, it rose brilliant and red. It was like the rising Sun she had seen in her vision when her friend Rose Marie died. Everything felt full circle—birth, death, and rebirth. She even remembered the women's prosperity circle and prayed that it would work out for all of them. Her new internet friends had become important to her. She prayed for her old friends, knowing how much they cared and loved her. She prayed for her sister and the next chapter for her family. She even prayed for her country to come together. She felt the vibration of the drums and songs penetrate her body. She surrendered to the truth and integrity of the beauty before her.

Frances's soul was present, front and center with her Creator, the Creator of a thousand names and a thousand places. Tears rolled down her cheeks, coming from a place of pure bliss and joy—joy to be so alive, to be so vibrant, to be so happy there in the arbor.

She realized how necessary this prayer gathering was for all the living on Earth. How the men and the women of the ceremony had sacrificed their comfort zone to pray for her and for all peoples—for the four-leggeds, two-leggeds, the creepy-crawlers, the finned, the furred, and the feathered. How ordinary, everyday people honored this tradition—instead of the robed, the righteous, the authoritarian order of things.

Although she was a Coastal native, this ceremony made her realize that native people of the Americas were descendants of that Pleistocene place called Beringia. That she was related to them all. That she belonged after all.

This is why she felt so honored to be invited here. Because, despite all the erasure of colonialism, this Sundance ceremony had survived. The Lakota had kept the spark alive for centuries. It had its own special voice and sense of belonging to this continent they called Turtle Island. Like the spirit of the ceremony, it was something Frances had been seeking for herself for seven decades.

This was the autumn of her life. It was time for her to let go of things that hindered her growth. Even at this age, there were lessons to learn about herself. The beliefs that sustained her when she was young were no longer working for her now. She had become a stubborn woman; she'd developed a point of view of knowing more than anyone else because of her age. Yet, she didn't understand the resistance and friction of her righteousness showing up here at the ceremony. She just didn't know what the correction within her was. This wasn't the woman of grace she had pictured as her older self. She prayed to make room for that possibility.

Over the past few days, Frances had witnessed some of the most beautiful colors in the sky. Squalls of rain would pass through sometimes in the afternoon, enough to cool everyone down from the summer's scalding presence. Vibrant rainbows would follow and then disappear in the breezes.

During those few days, she had felt her aloneness in the quiet times. She was comfortable by herself, wandering around the larger camp area doing her thing, exploring the fields of wildflowers, looking down prairie dog holes, washing the pots and pans, tidying up around the general kitchen area, and visiting with Yvonne and Tia at their tent sites in the evening. Yvonne's friend Theodore had made a habit of joining them for afternoon coffee since he had come to Frances's aid with the flat tire. They would take a walk, and Theodore would ask her about herself. She found it flattering that he wanted to know about her travels, her experiences, her world. Even though she wasn't looking for a new relationship, she couldn't help but find him attractive. He was stout and firm, as she felt when she tripped in a prairie dog hole and fell to the ground and he lifted her up like a feather. She knew he was younger than she was, and because of this, she resisted flirting with him. She just wanted to be his friend.

The sisters had become aware of her struggles with Doyle and the crew, as well as the grief she was carrying for the loss of her sister and close friend. They reminded her that she was there for healing, that the sweat lodge was for purification to unravel what kept her from growing and healing—that the Sundance ceremony was working on her behalf, for her highest and best.

She watched the people she had come with, feeling that she was growing further away from them and their activities. She felt that all the food, fuel, and supplies they had brought were being wasted because Doyle's strict, so-called protocols did not allow his camp to interact with or get close to the residents of Pine Ridge. They'd been told to work and to cook, yet it seemed to Frances that not much was getting done. How could they help the general kitchen if there was no communication? How could they know what was needed?

One of the previous days, she'd been sitting outside her truck when a Lakota boy camping with his family approached and asked her whether he could borrow some salt for his grandmother's stew. Frances had forgotten to pack some, but she knew there was plenty in the camp kitchen and lifted her chin in that direction. From where she was sitting, she'd been able to hear Doyle tell the boy no, that everyone was responsible for bringing their own supplies. This made

Frances mad beyond boiling, and she felt she had to say something about it. Yet, there was another part of her that said that's not what she had come all this way for. She had come to find healing from her grief at the loss of her sister, to find healing from her sorrows over the Earth's condition, and to continue her process of decolonizing herself. The last thing she'd wanted was to be angry.

Or so she thought, so she'd buried it.

The tipi had eventually been erected with the help of one of the tribal members while Doyle was gone. When Doyle did show up in the afternoons, he appeared shiny and showered, while his crew members were a bit crusty from camping. Doyle was supposed to participate in the ceremony as a dancer, but in his absence in the preparations of the ceremony that she witnessed from the other dancers indicated to her that he wasn't going to dance. He skipped out on the purification ceremony and making sage hoops for their regalia.

Doyle was different from the man she had known eight years before. At that time, he had shown more respect for women—and more respect for himself. She found it ironic that he limped around complaining about his injured knee, and there they were with the people of Wounded Knee. The more she'd watched him throughout the week, the more Frances had lost respect for him—and when Frances lost respect for someone, there was no turning back in her heart. Rarely did she give second chances because what she saw was what she got. She glimpsed for a second that he might be her mirror reflection because he triggered her so much. She didn't want to be like him because his ego was too big, she felt. Perhaps she wasn't egotistical enough? Perhaps she could learn from him to bring this into balance for her. Either way, she didn't like him.

Before breakfast that morning, Doyle walked around the tents announcing another meeting. Frances felt like this was a good morning to make some changes. She gathered herself and walked over to their common shade structure. Someone had made a fresh pot of coffee in the kitchen area, and she ran back to her truck to get her cup. When she returned, he had begun the meeting without her. Frances listened until it sounded like he was finished. She faced the crew and simply asked if this circle would commit to offering everyone a voice. In order to be unified with all circles, it was important to be unified *within* a circle. In a unified circle, everyone has a voice and everyone is accountable—including the circle's leader.

"The reason I bring this up," Frances said, "is because I've noticed a tension that exists here. I feel that if everyone had a voice, a lot of our problems could be solved. I only hear one voice—Doyle's. We all have something to offer each other during this short time. At least that's the women's way I was taught. The circle is supposed to be inclusive, not exclusive. When everyone honors each other's voice, there is balance. I mean, unity—isn't that why we are here?" She gestured toward the women standing together, inviting them to now add their voices to the conversation. She studied their faces to see if any of them had the courage to confirm her women's teaching. None of them looked enthused.

Not one spoke up; they just looked at her. Doyle spoke into the silence, stating, "There's no tension here. Right?" He gestured around the circle, seeming to invite opinions when he was really inviting everyone to agree with him.

"You see, Frances?" he said, "You are incorrect."

Frances could feel the itch of flames beneath her feet. "No, I am correct," she retorted. "I know the teachings. I know tension when I see it. I also know that there is tension within *me* when I see an elder denied bottled water or a child denied a couple of tablespoons of salt shared from our kitchen. Bread is going bad because we are not sharing." She glanced around the circle and saw that everyone looked like an anvil had rolled on their toes.

Doyle was focused on Frances. "You have never been here before," he told her. "I understand that. That's why I've given everyone here months to prepare for this ceremony. I know what I'm talking about. You don't."

Everyone seemed to stand in a stunned silence as the meeting broke up. Doyle had gathered a few women aside to talk about his drive to Rapid City. *Sure,* Frances thought as she walked away. *He has to have the last word.*

Frances's ways might not have been appreciated by Doyle and his crew, but the Lakota women had noticed that after meals, she would simply start washing the dirty pots without asking or needing to be asked. This way there were always clean pots and pans when it came time to start preparing the next meal. She could see what needed to be done, and they appreciated it.

This morning, as Frances finished washing up after breakfast, a Lakota woman she recognized as the head cook approached her. "We have some donuts someone donated," the woman said. "The coffee is still hot. Come sit with us for a bit." Frances could see that the woman had beautiful, dark skin and a chiseled nose underneath her baseball cap. Her features were formed from the beauty of her ancestors. The other women there also had beautiful faces that reflected their lineage.

"Oh, yes, I love donuts and coffee!" Frances said.

"Yeah, you always take off after you finish here," said the woman.

Frances smiled and lifted her chin toward the arbor. "I go down to the arbor. I just appreciate being here."

"Is this your first time?" asked a woman with long, thick braids extending from a blue cotton bandana tied around the crown of her head.

"Yes, I've never been to Pine Ridge before," Frances answered as she peeked into the box of donuts, then added, "Oh, these are the good bakery donuts."

They all laughed together.

"Well, you know we have to ask where you are from," said the head cook. "Aren't you with that group? They say they are from Washington."

Frances found her favorite kind of donut and set it next to the cup of coffee someone had placed in front of her. She felt this inquiry was different, that it came from genuine curiosity—as opposed to the Texan woman at the hot springs, who had been driven by a desire to make her feel different. Sometimes, the exact same question can carry a different weight or meaning. The Texan woman had made her feel like she was alien, an outsider, when she wasn't. "No, from California, actually. I was invited by that group to come here. I drove on my own, though."

The woman with the braids seemed surprised. "You drove all alone?"

"Yeah, took Interstate 80," Frances answered. "Days are long, you know."

Another woman wearing a lavender T-shirt continued the inquiry. "Do you have family?"

"I'm single," said Frances. "I just lost my only sister. She died of Covid recently. That's why I'm here."

All together, the women felt her words and soothed her with their words of condolence. One of them reminded her that on the last day, a feast would take place. She said they would need all the help they could get. As they continued to chat, Frances heard the sound of the drum and the singers. This meant the next round of the ceremony was beginning. She excused herself and walked a few steps before turning around to ask, "Hey, did anyone hear the buffalo the other night come through our camp?"

In response, the women just smiled at her and at each other. Frances wondered if they believed her.

Walking away from the kitchen, Frances began to recognize she was reaching the zone on the perimeter of the arbor—a zone of reverence. She switched gears, finding a spot between cars to slip off her skirt that was wet from washing dishes and slip on the ribbon skirt she loved. Out of her tote bag she pulled the prayer shawl she'd made herself, with intention and prayer in every stitch. She slipped it over her shoulders, grabbed her bag, and continued toward the arbor.

The drum songs escorted her into the sacred hoop of life. She had not become the Sundancer for Doyle's group like he'd wanted. She was glad she'd followed her intuition and told him no. As she had spent time with the Oglala people, she had been humbled by their presence and their dedication to the Creator. It had become clear to her that even with preparation, one does not just walk in without earning respect—which might take years to gather. Her participation on the outer circle of this ceremony was powerful enough, and it filled her eyes with tears of gratitude.

There was something special, something divine here that she had not felt before. She greeted her newfound friends with a quiet nod and began to step in unison with the community of prayers. Frances loved that feeling, yet something was vexing her. Thoughts of Doyle floated to the surface of her consciousness, and Frances decided to go down that rabbit hole. Memories of being mansplained and gaslit earlier led her to the anger she had buried.

When the round of drumming ended, she decided to take a short nap or be in the quiet of her tent in order to process her anger. She figured it wouldn't harm anyone or anything if she could be alone, in private. She began to walk toward her tent. She had just crossed the gravel road when two of the women from the crew—Megan and a younger woman with large breasts—approached her and gathered on both sides, leaning into her arms with their shoulders. In hushed, conspiratorial tones, they began to tell her to watch what she was saying.

"Be careful about what you say to local Oglala families around here," Megan warned Frances.

"There is word that you are telling them we sleep with Doyle," the younger woman added.

Next, Megan chimed in again: "It's important to apologize to Doyle. Do you understand?"

Frances stopped short in her tracks and began to rub her thighs in order to ground herself in her body and get some detachment from what the two women were saying. She was shocked at first because sleeping with him was the first thing they brought up; it seemed to confirm her suspicions. She remembered mentioning to the Lakota sisters her thoughts about the group's cult-like ways and that it may have come around to Megan. "First of all," she shot back, "I'm not apologizing to Doyle! Second, if he has a problem with me, why doesn't he tell me himself? Besides I don't need to talk or gossip about Doyle! You don't think people around here know what is going on? They ain't stupid. They don't need me to tell them he has tight control over you. Look at you, coming to fight his battles!"

All the things Frances feared about losing her temper were front and center now. The dread, the excitement, the regret, the fearlessness, the passion, the need to smack someone down were all there, present and available to her. Yet, she still was reluctant to cause a scene, so she walked away from the women, continuing in the direction she'd been headed when they'd approached her. She figured she'd said enough.

The two women followed her as she walked away from them, insisting that she apologize. Frances turned around and confronted them, locking her eyes onto theirs and saying, "Listen. Listen up, bitches. I've had enough of men like that! Like the men you see in the news, the so-called leadership of this nation. I'm sick of them telling me I'm wrong and they are right. Doyle is just another one of them. Do you understand? I don't want them around me. Besides, a good man would never ask me to do something they were not willing to do themselves. The good men I know would not blame me for things that went wrong while they were in charge. My father, my uncles, my cousins, my male friends are good men! They show respect toward women. Now get out of my face!" As she sped up her steps to walk away from them, she noticed her hands shaking. She was mad and she didn't want to be, but she allowed it to flow through her. Anger was not what she wanted to bring to her Sundance experience. She wanted this experience to be *kumbaya*, yet she couldn't seem to avoid her anger. There it was, like a volcano erupting and spitting out its hot lava, finding a way to correct itself within her.

This time, they didn't follow her. Frances felt a powerful

breakthrough as she walked alone toward the open prairie. A sense of trust returned to her. She finally, *finally* recognized the good men of her life—the men she had mentioned to Megan and her partner in crime. This was what had been missing from her perspective on the selfishness of men who claimed to be big leaders in the news—the men who lied in their hearings to become Supreme Court Justices, the men who gaslighted the insurrection, the men who disrespected women and laughed about it. When the pandemic reduced relationships to taking place through the computer, she had stopped having interaction with real men until her relationship with Doyle had presented itself. No wonder she was so fucking mad.

She began to laugh at herself for being so *pendeja.* The gentlemen she had wished for existed all around her; she had become so myopic that she didn't even see them. Masculinity could be righteous after all. She'd been blind to this and felt that blindness crumble off her eyes. She was seeing good men now because there were excellent men out there and she knew them.

The power of the men of the Sundance had come through for her by witnessing their commitment and sacrifice to pray for health and balance in everyone and everything. They were the unsung heroes, taking care of injustices in a quiet way—serving their communities and making sure the elders were warm, the children were fed, and the women felt safe. These men held true to their oath to serve their country's promise of unalienable rights. They led by example with their work ethic. Her father had been one of these men, and she had missed him so much since he'd died a decade ago. Her thoughts turned to Theodore, another protective man who cared. Where was he? She knew he was probably around somewhere helping out. She knew she would see him again before she left.

Theodore was a mystery to her. He seemed so gentle, yet very manly. He, too, wore long braids with a grey cowboy hat and Wranglers with neckbeads peeking out of his T-shirt. He was quiet. He listened. He smiled a lot. She remembered how they had met when she was standing outside of her truck trying to figure out how she was going to change her tire. Without hesitation or excuses, he'd parked his truck behind hers, introduced himself, and started to gather the tools he would need. She was a bit embarrassed by her situation, but he assured her that all was well. He even offered to get her tire repaired and asked her who she was staying with because he knew she wasn't from the rez. He recognized Yvonne's granddaughter, who was waiting with her next to the disabled car. He seemed to know everybody there.

His qualities were so different from Doyle and other men who had disappointed her. On one of their prairie walks, they had talked about the protocols of the ceremony, about the women dressing with modesty and not being able to attend during their moontime. He had told her she would have to decline if she was ever on her moontime. She'd laughed and said she was way beyond the moon-time years of womanhood. She had thought the respect she detected when he spoke to her was because he respected her as an elder; she was surprised to hear him say with sincerity that age didn't matter to him, and anyway, he had thought they were about the same age.

She wondered why this man had seemed to come out of left field. What was the significance of the appearance, at this particular time, of a solid, confident, secure man who wanted to become her friend—without asking for anything, without belittling her, without needing to brag about himself, but simply seeming to enjoy her presence? Did this mean she could love better?

# SERPENT MOTHER'S MEDICINE

It was the last day of the ceremony. Time felt suspended to Frances—the minutes, the hours, the days not seeming to pass in a normal way as she witnessed the layers of ceremony unfold before her. She understood why cameras were not allowed: because they froze time. This sacred time needed to flow uninterrupted. This ceremony was all outdoors, and the sky was the limit. The participants gracefully held their strength and endurance in service to mankind, womankind, childkind. All were included here. Her body would buzz with a deep respect and reverence for the Creator. It was good for her soul, her mind, her body, and her spirit.

The ceremony ended by noon on this final day, with everyone feeling grateful for another rotation around the Sun. Frances planned to stay another day or two to help break down the camp. She wanted a quiet moment to process the whole ceremony before helping in the big kitchen. As Frances started to walk toward her truck, she noticed the winds had picked up. She was feeling heavy with emotion. Something was vexing her again. She crawled into her tent and began to cry. She had managed to avoid Doyle these past days. She saw his tent and belongings, but it looked like he hadn't slept there at all. She heard him mention that his back and knees were bothering him; he was probably staying in the trailer house in a comfortable bed, with plumbing and kitchen comforts. It was all fine with her; he wasn't in her space. It wasn't until she'd seen him at the closing part of the ceremony that her sadness arrived—not anger, but sadness.

She had wanted Doyle to be something he wasn't. He wasn't the medicine man she had hoped for—a man of wisdom, a man of compassion. She had hoped that he would guide her to the grandmothers of Women's Ways, but it had actually been in spite of his efforts that she had found them in her new friends. She realized she had ignored the red flags and had not taken the time to really get to know him. She'd been so focused on her own agenda once she'd decided that this event would allow her to heal from her grief, embrace her anger, find a sense of belonging, and decolonize from the effects of sexism, ageism, racism, and all the other isms attached to the generations past. As Frances realized all this, her crying turned to deep sobs. As she picked up a discarded T-shirt lying in the corner of her tent and used it to wipe her wet face, an overwhelming dread entered her space.

This dread seemed to have to do with her being asked to accept toxic masculinity and all the external bullshit in the world. When she called it out, no one seemed to change other than her. She understood it all now and cried out to Changing Woman and all the spirit guides who had shown up in her dreams and journey visions—White Shell Woman, Tonantzin, White Buffalo Calf Woman. "Why? Why me? Why can't I just accept Doyle as he is? Why can't I accept what toxic males do to this country of mine? So many others accept their rules! Why can't I?"

Frances closed her eyes and felt the presence of Changing Woman offering an answer: "Because you are a warrior woman, and this is what warrior women do. They stand up strong for the unbalance between men and women. The others have seen you as a strong woman. They have watched your courage."

It fit. The message fit like a firm, comfortable boot. It was who she was, who she had always been, who she would be from now on. She was that *one* in the dreams. She was that *one* from her visions. She was that *one* in the mythical stories that she wrote about. She was that queen, that goddess, that divine femininity. She was that *one* if she was willing to change the perceptions of herself and see who she really was. If she was willing to wear her spiritual shoes and walk proud with her spirit name. She was *Yaguara Azul* because she was a warrior woman.

She wasn't an angry elder after all; she was strong, graceful, and beautiful. The ceremony worked its ways through her; it heard her doubts, her regrets, her sanity. It made her understand her deepest emotions and the shadows that lay hidden from her.

The wind began to push harder against the fabric of her tent, and she realized it might be best to take it down immediately. She climbed outside and began to disassemble it. She got it down and stuffed it neatly into the bag with ease in spite of the wind. The winds were strong and steady as she began to pack her camp supplies into the back of her truck. She glanced over toward the camp kitchen in the distance and saw them also packing up. She had promised to help, but she wondered if the feast would be canceled because of the wind. At that moment, a tent with its poles intact rolled by on a horizontal current that also carried other debris from the surrounding campsites.

Frances felt that all the cement of sadness was breaking off of her, including the last vestiges of her repressed anger, her sorrows, her arrogance—all of it had become an amalgamation of heavy energy attached to her. It was being blown off her body as she stood there exposed to the forces of nature. Her heart was racing as she let go of the stone walls she had built around her heart in order to feel safe. All of it was unraveling for her to feel the birthright of her liberty. The powerful winds of change had arrived, and it felt great to her.

She began walking with a new, strong stride toward the kitchen to help, but when the sound of the winds grew into a deep roar, she knew it would be impossible to serve food. She lost sight of the kitchen in the dust flying around and found it too dangerous to go any farther. She turned around and saw that her truck was beginning to disappear in the wind.

The skies became opaque with the topsoils of the plains, and yet Frances was able to discern a figure walking in the distance. She recognized the plaid shirt. It was Doyle. He was seeking shelter from the wind next to a railroad container nearby.

She felt like this was an opportunity to confront him at last, to give him a piece of her mind. She could not just let it go—so she ran over to him. When she came up close to him and touched his chest, she could see that it startled him.

She had every intention of telling him off, yet what came out of her mouth surprised her. In a loud and clear voice, she said, "Doyle, I need to tell you this. I need to tell you where I'm from. I'm from *La Cultura*—a place that taught me to respect others, to respect elders, but also to hold respect for myself. To stand tall and proud of being the indigenous Chicana I am and all it has taught me. I'm a warrior woman who will defend this practice of dignity. That is my medicine." This time, she was the one not pausing until she was finished. "You see, along the way, I forgot those parts of me. You pushed every trigger I have. But because of you, I was able to learn the lessons I needed. It's been a school of hard knocks, let me tell you." She found within her those heartfelt words and knew she would be able to say to him with sincerity. "Thank you. I only hope that you, too, find the lessons in our relationship."

His eyes had been locked on hers, but when she finished, he silently turned away, then walked to the edge of the container, leaving the windbreak. She watched as the cloud of dust swallowed him. She knew she would never have reason to see him again.

Her knees buckled, and she sat down next to the container. Her hair became entangled in the wind. Dirt sandblasted her face and tugged at her clothes. This hot summer wind was forceful as it blew around her, untangling her walls of self-protection. She recalled that her mother had once told her that her name, Frances, meant *free*. Most dictionaries would tell you it came from an ancient word for French people, but the true meaning in Latin went one layer deeper. She felt so vulnerable sitting there alone, yet the feeling of freedom—her namesake—felt as real as the prairie before her. Freedom filled her space, and the winds seemed to slither around her body like the great cosmic serpent Tonantzin. Freedom expanded, freedom blossomed, freedom exploded from within her. She cried warm, happy tears. She began to laugh in the warmth of the wind and sun. Dirt and dust entered her mouth, but she kept laughing anyway. The realization arrived that her heart had popped open.

Her mind had switched gears; her spirit was not restrained or held in check. She was free to change for the better.

All the distrust she'd had in men was gone. All the judgments she had carried around for so long about certain people had been lifted and carried away in the winds of change. She understood that it was *their* weight to carry, not hers. She placed her hands on her heart and felt its beat and rhythm strong and so alive. It was a big heart, a good heart, a sensitive heart, and a very generous heart. This freedom felt powerful to her, so powerful that in that moment, she felt she could consider loving again. Loving a man like Theodore, perhaps. She felt his kindness present within her own heart, followed by a sense of making room for possibility, of clearing the slate and allowing the seeds of her becoming to grow in the next chapter of her life.

In spite of the chaos, she felt calm and relieved in the grace and wisdom she had been looking for. It didn't matter whether or not Doyle heard her. What mattered was *her* truth. She had said it loud and clear. She was a mature woman, a crone, after all. It was *her* words that spoke of self-respect, *her* voice that was crystal clear. Like the silk of corn, *her* voice carried the pollen for the seeds of her tomorrows.

# REMEMBERING ME

Through the rain, the blizzards, the dust storms, I remain

A bit different than before, alchemy has taken hold

So I adjust to change as I lose bits and parts of me along the way

I know I must let go, but loss is so hard

When the winds cease and the dust settles

I'm in that quiet place

Remembering my heart

I ask who am I without those kindred, without enthusiasm?

My core exposed, I remember me

There is a formidable heart in there that remains

I am left here remembering me

– Frances Refugio Reyes

# acknowledgements

I have so much to be thankful for all the days of my life. First and foremost, for all the amazing *chingonas* that inspired me to write this book: I respect you for helping me to keep it real.

With much gratitude to the publishing team of Awaken Village who help make dreams come true. To Amanda Johnson: teacher, editor, book doula, chief inspirational officer—you are an honorary *chingona* in my book, astute as a publisher yet grounded and compassionate for all the creatives who come to you, including me. To Elizabeth Gudrais, my editor, I always wanted a teacher in my formative years who could guide me intellectually as you have done. Your kindness and ever-present patience provided that experience. Thank you. To Andrea Gibb, my designer and illustrator, thank you for listening and creating the vision I spoke about. Kirsten Stiegler, my marketing gal, love your enthusiasm.

To The Talking Book, Kris and Staff, thank you for helping oral storytelling stay alive. To Abbey West Recording, Jerry Spikula, your editing is impeccable. Thank you.

To my family: Robert A., my husband for many decades, *muchisimo amor* and gratitude for honoring my space and the time it took to create this. Together we dream big for this last quarter of our lives. My son, Damion, teaching me through your love since the day you were born to grow in profound ways. Marisa, my daughter, your strength and persistence amazes me. For my brother, Edward, and sister, Kathy, your love and support is always felt. My niece and nephews, Dylan, Derek, and Danielle: How you inspire me with your love and integrity. Marc, my nephew: You provided me with an important tool (a new computer) when I needed it the most—as well as with love from your family. With loving respect to Jennie Estrada, my siSTAR for keeping me alive when my lights were low. I made it to the finish line! To my cousins, who share their hearts. To my ever-present ancestors who whisper to me in the wind.

To my friends, my besties, my homies, my sisterhood: You know who you are because we speak the language of love and beyond. You laughed and cried with me. You pushed me forward in a wheelchair and you lifted my spirits when I was too weak to hold my head up. Your visits, your phone calls, your helping hands, your compassionate voices, and your beautiful hearts are weaved into my heart forever and ever.

To those beyond the veil, my spirit guides who know me better than I know myself: You make my existence adventurous and my heart happy.

*about the author*

Lorraine Martinez-Cook, Chicana Apache, was born and raised in Los Angeles. She moved to Indonesia in the nineties and began trekking across several continents. She currently lives in the Lake Tahoe region with her husband, Robert, and their dogs, Kiko and Danny. For many years, she was mentored as a medicine keeper of the North and South American traditions. An activist on issues relating to the Earth, women's rights, and Native American boarding schools, she was recently awarded a Senate Certificate of Recognition as a volunteer at the Stewart Indian School Cultural Center. She co-authored *Yo También: Stories of Hope and Healing* with a dynamic group and became a commissioned artist at Burning Man. She loves to dance to reggae and rap.

To learn more, find her on: awakenvillagepress.com/lorraine-martinez-cook or go to Instagram @lorraine.m.cook.3 or Facebook @The Sierra'ness Way.

www.ingramcontent.com/pod-product-compliance
Lightning Source LLC
Chambersburg PA
CBHW032222190726
48289CB00007BA/2354